The Invisible Staircase

The Invisible Staircase

A Novel by

Cathleen Claussenius

Moonlit Mile Publishing
Portland, Oregon

www.moonlitmilepublishing.com
www.theinvisiblestaircase.com

First Edition: August 2020

Library of Congress Control Number: 2016905552

Summary: When twelve-year-old Thea vows to solve the mystery behind a family
tragedy, she discovers an invisible staircase hidden high in a willow tree.

1. Middle Grade—Fiction. 2. Friendship—Fiction. 3. Grief—Fiction.
4. Children Flying—Fiction.

ISBN-10: 0997450517

ISBN-13: 978-0-9974505-1-4

For children, one to one hundred,
May you find the magic that you seek.

Table of Contents

Angela

*D*on't spill it," I said, handing Sam the styrofoam cup brimming with hot cocoa. I hurried out of the cafeteria and stepped into the Southern California sunshine.

"Thea, wait," Sam called.

Where is she? I thought as I scanned the crowd of kids.

Sam caught up with me. "Who are you looking for?"

"I told you already—the new girl. She's supposed to start today. Mrs. Fisher said so."

"Why do you want to find her?" Sam persisted.

I ignored him. Little brothers were so annoying. I had two big reasons to look for the new girl: 1. Whoever she was, when she got here, she would take my place as the newest sixth grader at this dog-doo school, and 2. Maybe she'd be cool, and maybe she'd be my friend.

Across the courtyard, I saw Jessica. As usual, she was flanked by Crystal and Claire. I called them the three-headed monster (just to myself) because they moved as if they were one animal (with three heads), never stepping even one foot away from each other.

Jessica was talking to someone sitting at a lunch table. *Dang it!* I thought. *Did Jessica already find her? She's going to contaminate her with her meanness, or worse, she might make her part of her monster unit, and I won't even get a chance to be her friend.*

I ditched Sam and pushed my way through the crowd, using my left arm to shield my cup of hot cocoa. When I was close, I heard Jessica say, "Welcome to Mar Vista Elementary—the best, and only, elementary school in Mar Vista."

The new girl sat at the end of the table, her golden hair shimmering in the sunlight. "Thank you," she said.

"So, what's your name?"

"Angela," the girl replied.

"Where you from?" Jessica asked sweetly.

"I am from Boise, Idaho," Angela said.

"Oh yeah, Idaho. Like Idaho potatoes," Jessica said. Crystal and Claire snickered. "When my mother buys potatoes at the grocery store, they come in bags that say *Idaho* in big blue letters. Why do they grow so many potatoes in Idaho?"

"Idaho is the nation's biggest producer of potatoes," Angela answered. She didn't seem to get it that Jessica was messing with her.

When Jessica said, "So, are you a family of potato heads?" Crystal and Claire burst into laughter and their laughter spurred Jessica on. "What kind of name is Angela? Are you some kind of angel? Are you a potato-head Angel? A potato with wings?"

My heart started pounding. "You better shut up!" I blurted.

Jessica turned, surprised. "Oh it's you, the weird girl with the weird name—*The A*. You can't tell me what to do."

I wanted to dump my hot cocoa on Jessica's head, but I knew that could have burned her, and I'm not that kind of person. But—and I'm not sure how it happened—someone, just at that moment, bumped me really hard from behind, and my hot cocoa flew out of my hand and hit her in the chest, covering her blue dress with sticky brown liquid.

"You'll be sorry for that!" she screamed.

"I'm already sorry—sorry you're Jessica-the-Jerk," I shouted at her.

Some kids laughed, and the three-headed monster ran away. "And my name is Thea," I called after her.

Angela had stood up. She looked frightened. "The students here are quite ill-mannered," she said.

"It's mostly Jessica. She's a brat."

"My name is Angela," she said, offering her hand for me to shake.

"Yeah, I know," I said, shaking her hand. *I knew she would be cool,* I thought.

Just then the bell rang. "I have to go to my locker. See you in class," I said.

I made it to class just as the second bell rang and plunked myself down in my third-row seat. Angela was standing at the front of the room talking to my teacher, Mrs. Fisher.

I liked Mrs. Fisher. She looked like the Betty Crocker lady on the cake mix box. You had to like Betty Crocker.

She made good cakes. That's why her face was on the box. And Betty Crocker wore a pearl necklace, which I figured her husband had given her as a gift. And I figured he was nice too, and they went out a lot together, and she always wore her pearl necklace.

"Class, our new student has arrived. This is Angela Vanderlin," Mrs. Fisher said.

I already met her, I thought. *Heck, I rescued her from the three-headed-monster.*

"Let's each of us introduce ourself to Angela. First, say your name. Then say an adjective that begins with the same letter as your name. Who can remind us what an adjective is?"

Claire's arm shot up. "An adjective is a describing word. It gives more information about the noun."

"Exactly so," Mrs. Fisher said. As an example, my name is Mrs. Fisher. A word that describes me is *friendly*. *Friendly* starts with *f*, just as *Fisher* starts with *f*."

Mrs. Fisher started down the front row. *What should I say? Thea—thirsty? Thea— thorny? Thea—Thanksgiving? Wait! Is Thanksgiving an adjective? It's almost my turn!*

"Brian—brave!" the boy next to me said. The class laughed.

"Thea—thoughtful," I stammered.

"Thea—thick," Crystal said under her breath. Claire giggled.

Mrs. Fisher frowned. "Let's move on."

Just then the door burst open. It was Jessica. She handed Mrs. Fisher a note and said, "My mother brought me a different dress. I didn't like the one I was wearing."

"Just have a seat, Jessica," Mrs. Fisher said.

Jessica sat down hard, and her ponytail wagged like a dog's tail. Crystal and Claire leaned in and whispered in her ears. In a moment, it was Jessica's turn.

"Jessica—Japanese," she said. Jessica was not of Japanese descent.

"That is inappropriate," Mrs. Fisher admonished her.

"Sorry. Let me try again." Jessica grinned. "Jessica—Jewish!" Crystal and Claire giggled. Jessica wasn't Jewish either.

Mrs. Fisher's face went red with vexation. "Very inappropriate, Jessica. Go to the principal's office."

"But I just came from there," Jessica protested. She gathered her belongings and headed for the classroom door, saying over her shoulder, "Maybe I'll change my dress again." Everyone laughed except me, Angela, and Mrs. Fisher.

"Jessica—jerk," I muttered.

When school let out, I waited for Sam in the parking lot. He arrived with his new buddy, Tim. Sam and Tim were made for each other. Both were bratty and allergic to lots of stuff. Tim walked the opposite way home from us, so they waved goodbye at the gate.

"¡Vámonos!" Sam said.

"Wait! Let's see if Angela comes."

"Who's Ang—"

"She's the new girl, ding-a-ling. There she is!" I said. Angela had emerged from the covered corridor and was heading across the parking lot toward us.

"That's the new girl? I've seen her before," Sam said.

"What are you talking about?" I said, staring at him.

"She moved in next door," he said matter-of-factly.

"I didn't see her move in next door."

"I see lots of stuff you don't see. They had a humongous truck. Mommy said they have fancy furniture."

"Angela! Want to walk with us?" I called.

Angela skipped over. "Most definitely," she said.

"This is my brother, Sam. He's seven. He says you moved in next door."

"I'm almost eight. *¡Vámonos!*"

"We go to my grandmother's after school. Want to come?" I asked.

"I should ask Mother," Angela said, hesitating.

"Thea!" Sam whined.

"It's only a few blocks from here," I said.

"Very well. I will telephone Mother from your grandmother's home."

"We call my grandmother, *Mamac.* Her real name is Mary Ann MacRobert. You're so lucky to meet her. She's really nice. And she has really good food."

When we turned onto Monroe Street, I spotted the top of Mamac's gray hair. She was wearing her old pink sweater and kneeling on her gardening pillow, weeding the pillowy dichondra that made her front lawn soft and lush like a thick green carpet.

"Mamac!" I exclaimed.

"Pink," Angela murmured. She stared at Mamac's pink house, the pink camellias blooming under the front windows, and the Queen Elizabeth roses (also pink) that filled the flowerbeds.

I ran to my grandmother. Mamac's knees crackled as she struggled to stand. "Oh, my poor knees," she said.

I hugged her around the middle. The soft cotton of her sweater felt nice against my cheek.

"This is Angela," I said.

Mamac pushed a wisp of gray hair from her face with the back of her gloved hand and gazed intently at my new friend. "Hello, Angela. Any friend of Thea's is welcome here. How are you, dear?"

"I am very well, thank you. How do you do?" Angela offered her hand, and Mamac removed her gardening glove to shake it.

I felt proud of Angela's good manners.

"She says it's all pink," Sam said. I stepped on his foot, and he cried, "Thea! What the heck?"

"Your home is lovely," Angela said, blushing.

"Mamac loves pink," I said. "Mamac, tell her why."

"When I was a little girl, I was not allowed to wear pink because my mother said pink was my sister's color. My color was blue. Now that I'm all grown up, I can choose what I like, and I choose pink!" She chuckled. "Now, let's go make snacks. You children must be hungry."

Inside, Angela called her mother (on the pink phone in the kitchen). I could easily imagine what her mother was saying.

"But I did not know I would be invited. . . . Yes, I am still wearing my school clothes. . . . I promise I will not get them dirty. . . . I met her today at school. . . ." Angela turned her back to me and lowered her voice. "It is a house. I do not know how big . . . Her grandmother and her brother . . . He is seven." When she said, "But they are nice people . . . ." I glanced at Mamac, but she was cleaning the counter and didn't look up. Then Angela said, "She is right here." She turned to Mamac. "Mother would like to speak with you."

Mamac took the phone. She was very polite to Angela's mother. After she hung up, she said, "You may stay until five thirty. That's when Thea's mother arrives. She will drive you home."

Angela's mother sounds so strict, I thought. Mamac won't say anything about it. She always tells us, "If you don't have something nice to say, don't say anything at all."

Mamac went to her pink refrigerator and came back holding a loaf of homemade bread. "Would you girls like to go out front and lasso an avocado off that old tree?"

I led the way out the back door. The avocado pole was leaning against the garage. It was old and splintery and had an empty coffee can nailed to one end. We carried it down the driveway to the front of the house where the avocado tree grew near the front steps.

"There's one," I said, pointing. We maneuvered the pole straight up and lifted it high. Then we bumped and jiggled until the avocado fell into the can.

"Perfect," Mamac said when we delivered the bumpy black fruit. She cut it in half and whacked the pit with the blade of her knife to pull it out. Then she scooped the green goodness from each half and mashed it with a fork onto two pieces of toast and sprinkled them with garlic salt. Sam sat at the counter eating an apple and watching.

"Would Samuel like some?" Angela asked.

"Oh no," I said. "He's allergic to avocados. He

wheezes, and his lips get fat. Sometimes he gets asthma. Sam, tell Angela what you're allergic to."

"Avocados, strawberries, honey, smog, dust, cigarette smoke, cat hair, dog hair . . ." Wet apple bits sprayed from his mouth as he spoke, and he started to laugh.

"Here you go, girls," Mamac said, handing me the platter with the scrumptious treats. "Take the quilt from the porch, and you may sit under the willow if you'd like."

I grabbed the quilt, and we followed the brick path through the garden, past the towering Queen Elizabeth roses (yes, they were in the backyard too), and around the back of the garage to the clothesline. Here the path ended, so we cut across the dichondra to the willow tree which stood in the very back corner of the yard.

The willow's leaves swept the ground like a grass hula skirt. I pushed them aside, and we laid out the rosebud quilt and sat cross-legged. I took a big bite of my avocado toast. Angela nibbled hers.

"Don't you like it?" I asked.

"We do not eat many avocados in Idaho and never on toast with garlic salt. It is different but savory," she declared. She held her free hand underneath her toast like a plate. "If I stain my school clothes, Mother will be angry."

I gobbled up my snack and finished Angela's for her. "I love this tree," she said, gazing up into the crisscrossed branches silhouetted against a brilliant blue sky.

"Me too," I said. "It's like a person. See how the limbs reach out all crazy like crooked fingers?"

"Yes. Other trees do not do that," Angela said.

"If I were a bird, I'd land on that highest branch and sing to the clouds," I said.

"And then fly away," Angela added dreamily.

"Down here it's a secret room," I said, gazing at the shaggy layers of narrow leaves that formed a circle around us. I lay on my side and propped my head up on one arm. "Why did you move to Los Angeles?"

"My father is a lawyer. He helps corporations pay less taxes. They gave him a big promotion, and we had to move here." She sighed. "We have an apartment now, but it is temporary. Very temporary, according to Mother."

"How come?"

"We are building Mother's dream house in the San Fernando Valley. Do you know where that is? It is somewhere in Los Angeles, but you have to drive on the freeway to get there. Father promised he would build her dream house."

"That's nice of him."

"I suppose. Mother always wants to spend more and more and more. She says, 'I'll take a dozen in assorted colors.' She thinks she is humorous when she says that. They quarrel about it sometimes. Not about her saying that but about money."

"We used to live in a big house in the Pacific Palisades. That's in Los Angeles too. We went broke after my dad died. That's why we live in an apartment now, and that's why I had to change schools."

"Your father died?"

"Yeah—someone shot him."

Angela's eyes widened. "But why would someone do such a terrible thing?"

"At the funeral, Uncle Ray was crying and whispering over my dad's coffin. 'I'm sorry, Howie. I'm so sorry. It's all my fault.' That's what he said."

"Howie was your father's name?"

"His name was Howard, but Uncle Ray called him Howie. I told Mom about it. She freaked out and told the police. They talked to Uncle Ray, but he said I must have heard wrong, and he didn't know anything about what happened to my dad."

The confusion I'd felt since Dad's death returned. Now the avocado didn't want to settle in my stomach, and the garlic flavor in my mouth tasted gross.

"I miss my dad," I said and began to cry. Angela stared at me. Her beautiful blue eyes filled with tears, and I thought she might cry too. "Do you want to know my secret promise?" I asked her.

"I do."

"Someday, I'm going to find out who shot my dad, and he's going to pay for it."

Angela put her hand on my arm. "I hope you do, Thea. You know what?"

"What?"

"I am happy that we are friends."

Angela's words made the terrible ache I felt about Dad melt away. "Want to climb the tree?" I asked, jumping to my feet. "We can spy on the neighbors."

"That would be fun," Angela said. "Oh, I wish I were wearing my play clothes. I will have to take care."

The willow tree had two main branches that forked out and up from its massive trunk. Angela climbed the branch on the right, and I climbed the one on the left. When we were a ways up and at the same level, we peeked out through the leaves into the yard behind Mamac's. Mrs.

Oxford was hosing off her patio. Then her son came out, and they began to argue about him using her car. We covered our mouths and giggled.

When Mom arrived at five thirty, Angela said, "Thank you for having me Mrs. MacRobert."

"You are very welcome. And please call me Mamac."

We were out the front door when Angela ran back to give Mamac a hug. Mamac held her for a moment and stroked her hair. "You are always welcome here, dear," she said.

Mamac knew who needed love.

*I*t turned out that not only had Angela moved into the apartment building next door, but our bedrooms were both upstairs and right across from each other.

After school, Angela started going to Mamac's with me and Sam every day. We were like a family with three kids—from right after school until five thirty. Mamac was always glad to see us. She figured out that Angela liked plain food and made her tuna sandwiches with peeled carrot sticks on the side.

Mamac had a deep freezer on her back porch. Inside, she kept jars of homemade cookies: chocolate chip, walnut, oatmeal raisin, and anise seed. We'd grab handfuls on our way out the back door to the garden. We'd scale the willow tree and spy on Mrs. Oxford. Then we'd lay out Mamac's rosebud quilt and do our homework.

During the first weeks, Mrs. V (that's what I called Angela's mom, Mrs. Vanderlin) came over a bunch of times. She made an excuse to go into every room of the house.

"These older homes are so charming," she gushed, in her fake, *I'm-so-interested-in-you* voice. "Just look at the wainscoting! May I . . . ?" She put her hand on the doorknob of the spare bedroom.

"Of course. Please do," Mamac said graciously.

It was just Mamac's sewing room. A single bed took up most of the space. It was my room when I slept over.

One day Mrs. V sent play clothes with Angela so she could change into them after school. That's when I knew she had accepted us.

Stupid me. I thought we would go on like that forever.

Mamac

$\mathcal{M}$iss Schwaderer looked like the wicked witch from *The Wizard of Oz except her face wasn't green.* She was our school principal. Once, during lunchtime, Angela and I were goofing around, and Miss Schwaderer got it in her head that Angela had pushed me.

"Paper-pick-up for you, missy," she said.

Angela was so mortified, she couldn't speak. She never got in trouble. Miss Schwaderer stared at her over the rim of her glasses.

"I'll do it for her," Ricky said. (Ricky Kenton was the cutest boy in our class.)

"Well, that's fine, young fellow," Miss Schwaderer said. "Gallantry signifies strong moral fiber."

Angela went all gaga when Ricky took her paper-pick-up duty. She had a crush on him the size of Alaska.

None of it made sense to me. Angela hadn't pushed me. But, if she had, why should she pick up trash? And, if she should pick up trash, why was Ricky allowed to do it for her?

In June we were in the auditorium with Mrs. Fisher, rehearsing our graduation ceremony. Tomorrow was going to be my day—Thea MacRobert, sixth-grade graduate!

The door at the back of the auditorium opened, and Miss Schwaderer appeared.

Angela whispered, "How old do you think she is?"

"A hundred and two," I said. We giggled.

"It is blue dress day," Angela said. "She always wears her blue dress or her black dress."

"Maybe she only has two dresses."

Miss Schwaderer had reached the steps of the stage. She grasped the stair rail tightly as if it might try to wiggle away. When Mrs. Fisher saw her, she stopped speaking mid-sentence and rushed over.

"I think Mrs. Fisher is afraid of her," Angela whispered.

"She's not the only one," I whispered back. We stifled more giggles.

Miss Schwaderer said something to Mrs. Fisher, and Mrs. Fisher walked briskly to the microphone where she had been calling student names. "Thea MacRobert," she said.

"What did I do?" I trotted over to Mrs. Fisher. "Am I in trouble?"

"No, of course not, Thea. Go to the office with Miss Schwaderer. Your mother is coming to pick you up."

"Why? What's wrong?"

Miss Schwaderer walked over to where we stood. The whole class was watching.

"You are Thea MacRobert?" she asked.

"You don't know my name?"

"Thea, your grandmother is ill. Follow me please."

As I walked past Angela, our eyes locked.

"What is wrong?" Angela's lips silently voiced the words.

"Mamac," I mouthed.

I followed Miss Schwaderer down the stage steps. *She's as slow as a snail! Mamac is sick? I saw her yesterday. How can she be sick?*

When we got to the main office, Sam was sitting in front of the large picture window. I ran over and sat next to him.

"Hi," he said faintly.

This is like that other day, I thought. *The day Dad . . . We were called to the front office to wait for Mom. Is Sam remembering that day too? I could tell him not to worry. I could tell him everything will be okay, but it might not be true. Really bad things do happen sometimes . . . .*

Mom's white station wagon pulled up to the curb. Sam ran outside shouting, "Dibs on the front seat." I didn't bother to yell at him about that and got in the back.

"What's wrong with Mamac?" Sam asked Mom before I had even shut my door.

"She was gardening in her front yard and fainted. A neighbor called an ambulance."

"Is she okay?" I asked.

"I don't know anything, hon. I got a message at work. She's at Saint John's Hospital in Santa Monica. We'll know more when we get there."

We drove in miserable silence. I stared blindly out the

window.

At Saint John's, Mom parked the car, and we found our way into the massive, stony-white building and then to the elevator. "Push 5," Mom said to Sam. On the fifth floor a fat lady in a white nurse's uniform said, "Dr. Haserband wants to speak with you. Please have a seat."

We sat on plastic chairs and waited for what felt like an eternity.

Finally, a blond man in a white lab coat appeared. He had long legs and moved quickly toward us. Mom sprung to her feet. "Wait here," she said. Sam and I watched from our sweaty seats as Mom stepped away with the blonde man. When she returned, she said, "Let's go."

"Was that the doctor?" I asked.

"Yes."

"What did he say?"

"Honey, you know Mamac has a heart condition. Everything she's been through these last couple of years—to lose a son . . ." Mom looked away.

She's thinking about Dad—Mamac's son.

Mom started walking down the corridor as if she had forgotten we were there. We had to run to catch up. We found Mamac in room 516. She lay in bed—her eyes closed. There was a monitor next to her. A jagged green line went up and down. *Mamac's heartbeat . . .*

My throat ached.

"Here, honey," Mom said, offering me a chair. Mom held Mamac's hand. "Thea, Sam, and I are here," she said. Mamac's eyes stayed closed.

After a while, Mom said it was time to go.

Sam's face was a stone mask. He kissed Mamac's

cheek. "Bye," he said.

I took her hand. Her fingernails shone pink with polish. "Goodbye, Mamac," I said. *That sounds too forever!* "I'll see you soon." I kissed her cheek and could smell her sweet face cream.

Mom took us to Scott's Burgers for dinner. This was usually a special treat but not this evening. We didn't talk much, and my hamburger tasted as dry as sawdust.

When we arrived home, I felt super tired and went to bed. The next morning, my first thought was, *graduation day!* A delicious tingle raced through me. Then I remembered. *I hope Mamac is better today. I wish she were coming to my graduation. My dress!* Mamac had sewn me a special dress for this day. It was red and had a lace sash tied above the waist. She had told me this was called empire style. *We didn't pick it up yesterday after we went to the hospital. I guess Mom forgot. I forgot too . . . .*

Sam and I were eating Rice Krispies when Mom came into the kitchen.

"Thea, I'll meet you at the steps in front of the auditorium right after the ceremony. I have to go now. I can't be late for work again."

Mom grabbed her purse from the kitchen counter and started rummaging through it as she headed for the front door. "Where are my keys?" she muttered.

"Mom, wait! We forgot my dress."

"What dress?"

"My graduation dress. It's at Mamac's."

"I'm sorry, Thea. It can't be helped now." She ran back into the bedroom then rushed back into the living room and started searching amongst the newspapers and magazines stacked on the coffee table. "I just can't keep it all straight!"

"I can help," Sam said.

I watched as Mom and Sam moved faster and faster in frantic circles, searching.

Everywhere Mom looked, Sam looked too. "Look somewhere else, dufus!" I ordered. He disappeared down the hall.

A few seconds later, he burst back into the living room and leapt halfway across the floor. "Found 'em! In the bathroom!" he shouted, holding the keys triumphantly above his head.

At eight fifteen, Sam and I met Angela downstairs in the courtyard of Angela's apartment building. She looked great in her navy-blue dress. Her glossy-red belt matched her high-heeled sandals. I felt like a total dork standing next to her in my brown skirt and wrinkled white blouse.

"You look fab," I said.

"You know Mother. 'You must always look smart,'" she said, imitating Mrs. V's lilting voice.

"I have a new dress. Mamac made it for me. We forgot to pick it up from her house yesterday."

"Oh, Thea!" Angela said, grabbing my arm. "Tell me what happened. Mrs. Fisher said you had a family emergency."

I told Angela about our visit to the hospital.

"Father says there is always hope," Angela declared.

"He doesn't know anything about it and neither do you," Sam shouted. He took off running and disappeared around the front of the building.

"Sam!" I called, but he was gone.

"Poor little guy," Angela said.

"He's a dweeb," I said.

I walked through my graduation ceremony like a robot. I tried not to worry, but I couldn't help it. I kept thinking, *I wish Mamac were here.*

Miss Schwaderer made a speech, but I didn't hear one word of it. There was music. Our names were called. Then it was over.

Outside, I pushed my way through the crowd. I spotted Mom and ran to her.

"How is Mamac?"

"Let's talk about that at home," she replied.

"Why? Is she better? Is she worse? Tell me!"

"Yeah, tell me too," Sam chimed in.

"Not now. Let's go in and have refreshments."

We ate cookies and drank punch while eleven- and twelve-year-olds ran around and parents chatted. There was a lot of hugging and saying goodbye. I felt like I had just dropped in from Mars.

Back home, the second we were through the front door, I said to Mom, "Call the hospital now and find out how Mamac is."

Mom put a hand on Sam's and my shoulders and walked us to the couch. "I didn't want to tell you at your graduation. I didn't want to spoil it." She paused. "Mamac passed away last night in her sleep."

"What? You said . . . She died?" I gagged and ran to the toilet. I threw up three times—all the way down to the morning's Rice Krispies.

Sam didn't cry. He just sat and stared. Then his

wheezing started, and by dinner, he was having a full-blown asthma attack. Mom got his inhaler for the third time.

"Open up," she directed. Sam opened his mouth, and Mom sprayed the medicine into the back of his throat. "Breathe it in, hon."

The inhaler helped a little, but the wheezing kept coming back. At eight o'clock, we took him to the emergency room at Saint John's, and they gave him a shot. That helped a lot. The doctor wrote a prescription for a new kind of inhaler.

"You must carry this with you from now on, son," he said.

Sam stared at the doctor. "I'm not your son," he said.

"Sam, it's an expression. The doctor is trying to be friendly." Mom smiled weakly at the doctor. "We've had some family issues. He's just—"

"It's no problem," the doctor replied. "Sam, it's important that you carry your new inhaler with you. If you start wheezing, use it. That will keep your asthma from getting out of control."

*T*he Presbyterian church looked like one of those old-fashioned churches you see on Christmas cards—without the snow. It was surrounded by big trees and curved walkways. We hardly ever went there—just on Christmas Eve and Easter Sunday. On the day of Mamac's funeral, I thought, *Now we come here for funerals. First dad's and now Mamac's—our new family tradition.*

"Mamac had many friends," Mom said as we pulled into the parking lot crammed with cars. "Olive Dancer helped me notify everyone."

"How come she's called Olive?" Sam asked. "Is she an olive?"

"Right, Sam. She's an olive, a dancing olive," I said.

We parked and followed the crowd into the chapel. Pink rosebud bouquets had been placed at the end of each pew down the center aisle. Olive Dancer waddled toward us. I had never seen her in a black dress before.

"The bouquets are very sweet," Mom said.

"In honor of my dear friend," Olive Dancer said. "The woman walked to church every Sunday. God bless her."

"She believed in fresh air and exercise," Mom replied.

"A great lady," Olive Dancer said. "Always wore a hat to church—pink flowers pinned on top. She used to say, 'A lady never removes her hat!'"

"Thank you for all your help, Olive." Mom stepped forward to hug her, but Olive Dancer shrugged her off.

"I loved her—that's all," she said, dabbing her eyes with a lace handkerchief.

Mom led us to the front pew, and Sam asked, "Are we the only ones sitting up here?"

"The front pew is reserved for family," Mom said.

We're Mamac's only family? Wait a minute. What about Uncle Ray? He's Mamac's son. He could sit up here with us. He might even sit next to me!

"Mom, is Uncle Ray coming?"

"I can't imagine he would miss his own mother's funeral, but with him, you never know," she said stiffly.

I peered toward the back of the church. *I don't want him to sneak up on me.*

"Let us pray," Reverend Gilbert said. A hush went

through the chapel. I peeked over my shoulder again to look for Uncle Ray, but all I saw were the bowed heads of people praying.

At Dad's funeral, we sat in this same spot. Mamac held my hand.

"The Lord is my shepherd; I shall not want. He maketh me to lie down in green pastures—" Reverend Gilbert had bowed his head and was praying out loud.

At Dad's funeral, Uncle Ray sat in the back with his hippie-dippy girlfriend. She had long brown hair and wore a ton of green eye shadow.

Uncle Ray and the hippie drank from a bottle hidden in a brown paper bag. She kept hugging him. Reverend Gilbert talked just like he's doing now. Afterward, when everyone was leaving, Uncle Ray took daisies from the big vase next to Dad's casket and gave them to the hippie girl and kissed her hand.

Olive Dancer said, "What in heaven's name? Has he no respect?"

"Never mind," Mamac said. "There's no harm in it."

"That is no way to behave. Not in the Lord's house. Not on this day," Olive Dancer said.

Out in the parking lot, I asked Mom if I could get a daisy from the vase too.

"Of course you can, hon," she said.

I wanted Mom to go back into the church with me, but people were coming up and talking to her, and she kept walking toward our car. So, I ran back into the church by myself. I really wanted a daisy. I wanted to take it home and iron it between two pieces of wax paper. I wanted to keep it forever.

After being outside in the bright sunshine, I could hardly see inside the church. I didn't even see Uncle Ray till I got up front. He was standing by Dad's casket. His hands were on the shiny brown wood, and he was talking.

"I'm sorry, Howie. It's my fault. You were just trying to help me. Please forgive me . . . ."

I stopped halfway up the altar steps. I didn't know what to do. Should I take a daisy or wait until he went away? Then the hippie girl appeared. She practically danced down the aisle swinging her fringed-leather purse. She trotted up the steps to Uncle Ray and put her arm around his waist.

"Who's the kid?" she asked.

"What kid?" That's when Uncle Ray turned around and saw me standing behind him.

"Thea," he said, wiping his eyes. "I was just—I was saying goodbye—again."

I rushed forward and grabbed a daisy from the vase, then I ran away as fast as I could.

Later, lots of people asked about Uncle Ray. They said how sorry they were for him. I didn't feel sorry for him. He had a secret. A bad one. When I told Mom what Uncle Ray had said, she kept asking me, "Are you sure?" and, "What were his exact words?" Like I told Angela, Uncle Ray denied the whole thing, and there was nothing anybody could do because they had no proof.

I'm older now. I'm not afraid of Uncle Ray. He knows why Dad was shot, and somehow, I'm going to find out what he knows.

I shut my eyes tight and bowed my head.

Dear Mamac,
 Can you help me? I have to find out who killed Dad. I know Uncle Ray was your son and you loved him a lot, but Dad was your son too. Why did Uncle Ray say he was sorry and it was all his fault?
 And Mamac, I already miss you so much.
Amen.

I tasted salty tears and wiped my cheek with the back of my hand. Mom patted my knee.

"It's all right to cry, hon," she whispered. "It's a very sad day."

"Mary Ann MacRobert was loved so much because she gave so much love," Reverend Gilbert said.

"Amen to that," Olive Dancer said loudly.

I turned, and something caught my eye—a figure standing at the back of the chapel. My scalp tingled, and I stared straight ahead. *Is that Uncle Ray?* I waited as long as I could stand it, then I peeked. The figure was gone. *Probably just someone who works here . . .*

"Anyone wishing to do so may now pay their last respects," Reverend Gilbert said.

Hushed conversations began all over the chapel. A line formed at the altar steps. One by one, Mamac's friends walked up to her casket. Some just looked. Some spoke. A few leaned over and kissed her cheek.

"Mommy, are they kissing Mamac?" Sam said in astonishment.

"Yes, hon," Mom replied.

"Why is her casket open? Dad's casket wasn't open," I said.

"Mamac put it in her funeral instructions. That's the

way some people do it," Mom said.

"Where is Ray?" It was Olive Dancer. She stood in front of Mom with her hands on her hips.

"He may be here somewhere," Mom said, glancing around.

I didn't say a word about the figure at the back of the church.

Mom stood up and started toward the altar, pulling Sam along with her. I wanted her to slow down. *Is my Mamac really up there? I've never seen a dead person before* . . . . I imagined the skeletons from Halloween. *Will she look like that?*

At each end of the casket, there was a vase of pink carnations. As we got closer, their spicy smell filled the air.

A face—Mamac's face? Someone made her hair curly. Her hair should be fluffy. Her cheeks are red. They put makeup on them. Her lips! They're red too. Mamac wore pink lipstick. That's not her. It's just not her.

"Children, this isn't really our Mamac," Mom said.

"Who is it?" Sam asked.

"I mean, it is her body, but Mamac's spirit is in heaven. She's with God."

Sadness gnawed at my insides. I needed to cry, but I didn't want people to stare at me or try to comfort me, so I swallowed hard and pushed the crying beast down.

"Funerals are for the people left behind—a place to come together and remember their loved one," Mom said.

Mamac wore her rose-colored suit. She had sewn it herself. *That's what she wore to the tea party we gave in home economics class.* In my head, I could see her standing in the doorway of my classroom smiling in her suit and hat.

Then, out of the blue, Mom reached inside the casket.

"Mom! What are you doing? Don't touch her!" I said.

"Mamac wanted you to have her cameo." She unpinned the oval brooch from the collar of Mamac's white blouse. "She told me it is a MacRobert tradition that it be passed to the oldest female child."

"Is that me?"

"Yes, Thea. Mamac had no daughters, and Ray has no children, so you are the next girl in line."

Mom placed the cameo in my hand. It had the three-dimensional profile of a woman's face set on an amber-colored backing. Its oval edge was trimmed with twisted gold wire. It was very familiar to me. Mamac wore it to church and when she went out with her garden club.

I didn't notice the cameo was getting warmer until it was so hot, I almost dropped it. I looked at Mom, but she was talking to Sam. Prickly pins swept up my arm and into my chest. I didn't like it. I thought I was having a heart attack. Then the tingling stopped and so did the heat. A soothing current coursed through my veins—like a cool breeze at the end of a hot day. *It's love. Mamac is sending me her love through the cameo!*

"Thank you, Mo—" I didn't finish my sentence because a man with shaggy black hair and a bushy beard was walking toward us. He was behind Mom—only a few feet away—and she didn't know it. I couldn't warn her. I couldn't speak. My heart hammered. Uncle Ray!

The Cameo

*U*ncle Ray had come in the side door, pushing past a group of mourners who were leaving. Mom noticed my frozen stare and turned.

"Oh!" she exclaimed.

I stared at my uncle. *Gross. Wolfman. Beady eyes. Wild hair. The wolf won't even look Mom in the eye. He's staring at his dirty boots. Now he's peeking back at that door he just came in. He wants to run away. Run away, scary wolfman.*

"She was a beautiful person," Uncle Ray muttered, glancing sideways at the coffin.

Don't look at Mamac! my brain screamed, but I just stood there like an obedient dog. The tangy smell of carnations was gone now, replaced by the stink of Uncle Ray—stale and smoky.

"Say, Michelle. Got a smoke?"

"No, Ray. You know I don't smoke."

"Nah, I didn't know that." He paused. "I'll see you at the lawyer's."

"I need to drop off the chil—"

Uncle Ray had already turned away and fled the same way he had come in.

Back home, I put Poor Boy sandwiches in the oven for dinner. These were bologna and cheese on long sourdough rolls. They came frozen, two in a box. After baking for sixty-five minutes, the rolls got hot and crusty, like French bread. They were yummy, especially with the mustard from the packets that came in the box.

Sam sat at the kitchen table, fiddling with his matchbox cars. "Where's Mommy?" he asked.

"She went to the lawyer's to hear Mamac's will," I said.

"What's a will?"

"It's what a person wants done with all their stuff after they die. You write it down. Everyone has to do what it says."

"Is Mamac with Daddy?"

"Yeah. They're two angels in heaven. Now eat your food."

"I wish they were here where I could see them."

"Me too," I said. The achy sadness I felt at the funeral returned. I plopped into the chair across from Sam and burst into tears. Sam came over and put his arms around my neck, which made me cry even more.

"Don't be sad," he said. "They're two angels in heaven."

Mom's key clicked in the front door. When she saw Sam comforting me, she rushed toward us.

"My darlings!" She threw her arms around us. "Remember, we are a family, and we will always have each other."

We ate the Poor Boys, and Mom told us surprising news.

"Your Mamac loved you so much—she has left her house for us to live in until Sam graduates high school. She must have changed her will after your dad died. Bless her heart."

"We're going to live at Mamac's?" Sam asked.

"What about Uncle Ray? Will he be there?" I asked.

"No, honey. Don't you worry about him. He's going to receive money from Mamac's life insurance. When Sam graduates high school, we'll move out of Mamac's house, and it will be transferred to Ray permanently. He'll be fine." Mom sniffed and straightened.

"I would love to live at Mamac's," I said.

"Me too!" Sam said, bouncing up and down in his seat.

After dinner, we snuggled with Mom on the living room sofa. She opened an old photo album. "Mamac was super pretty," I said, pointing at a black-and-white photo of a young woman standing in the sunlight. Behind her was a mass of long, drooping leaves.

"Is that Mamac's willow tree?" Sam asked.

"Yes, honey. It was a grand tree, even back then. Mamac and Grandpa bought that house over forty years ago."

"I don't remember Grandpa," Sam said.

"That's because he died when I was four. You were a baby," I said.

"Your dad had brown eyes like your grandpa," Mom

said. "You both have your dad's eyes."

"Who's that?" Sam asked, pointing at a photo of a boy holding a baby.

"That's your daddy. He's about your age in that photo. The baby is Ray."

"That little baby is Uncle Ray?" Sam asked incredulously.

"Hard to believe, huh? Mamac always said he was a sweet baby," Mom said.

"How come he's so weird now?" I asked.

"Yeah, and smells bad," Sam added.

"It goes way back. Even in high school, I remember Ray hanging with the wrong crowd. He got into drugs and was expelled. He never did graduate."

"What did he do then?" I asked.

"He joined the Army. We hoped that would straighten him out, but they discharged him early—something to do with gambling. So he came back to L.A. but got arrested for cashing stolen checks and went to prison for a year. When your dad died . . ." Mom looked at Sam and stopped speaking. Sam didn't know about Uncle Ray whispering, "I'm sorry," and, "It's all my fault," over Dad's casket, and Mom wanted to keep it that way.

"Anyway, Mamac worried about him. He'd call her now and then to let her know he was all right and usually to ask for money."

"He's jeepers creepers," Sam said.

$\mathcal{L}$ater that night, when I was getting ready for bed, I stood at my dresser mirror and stared at my reflection. *Brown eyes, brown hair, brown mole above my lip.*

Brown, brown, brown. Brown bear. Brown dirt. Brown poop. I was still wearing the dark green dress I had worn to the funeral. I yanked off my belt. *Fat, fat, fat. Fat freak.*

I reached in my pocket and found the cameo brooch. *Doesn't feel hot now* . . . I pinned it to the front of my dress and checked the mirror. "Elegant," I said out loud. *But I won't ever wear it. It's for a grownup.*

Just then, my reflection began to blur as if water had washed over the mirror. I blinked. Golden light shone from the cameo pinned to my dress. My heart began to race.

The cameo is going weird again . . . . In the mirror, I could see blurry beams of gold and green light bouncing off the walls behind me. Some even ricocheted off my head.

Mom came in carrying Sam, and the spell was broken. I tried to act normal, but my hands were shaking. I picked up the silver, heart-shaped box Mom had given me for my birthday and dumped its contents into the top drawer of my dresser. Then I unpinned the cameo and nestled it inside the box.

"This boy is getting heavy," Mom huffed as she plopped Sam onto his bed. (Our apartment only had two bedrooms, so Sam and I shared.)

"Getting heavy," Sam mumbled, rolling onto his side.

"You kids are growing up fast," Mom said. She crossed the room and gave me a hug.

Before turning out my bedside light, I hopped onto my bed and peered out the window at the apartment building next door. Angela's bedroom light was still on. Months before, we had rigged up a looped nylon cord between our bedroom windows for sending notes back and forth. Now, a folded lavender paper gripped by a clothespin fluttered in the night air. I opened the window and snatched it off the line.

Dear Thea,
How are you? I feel sad about Mamac. I hope we can play tomorrow.
❀ Love, Angela ❀

I held the note to my heart. *My perfect Angela!* I liked that her closet was full of the nicest clothes. They were organized by function first: special occasion, school, play, and then grouped by color. Her top dresser drawer was filled with uniform rows of rolled tights, underwear, and matched socks. They reminded me of dinner rolls on a baking sheet.

I was scrawling a reply when I heard the muffled ring of the telephone. I didn't think anything of it until I heard a voice, low and terse. *Is that Mom?*

I checked on Sam. He was sound asleep. I slipped out of the room and down the hall. Mom's door was open. I crouched on the floor and peeked inside. She was sitting on the bed, talking on the telephone.

"Ray, calm down. What? . . . But the lawyer said you're getting ten thousand dollars from the life insurance. That is a lot of money. . . . Mamac wanted her grandchildren to grow up in a real house. Our rent here is so high, we're living hand-to-mouth. . . . I had no idea she was going to set it up this way. . . . Stop it, Ray. Don't speak to me like that. The bank controls the house now. We don't have the power to sell it even if we wanted to, and I don't want to. . . . Hello? Hello?"

Mom hung up and stared at the wall.

I crept down the hall and got back into bed.

Ricky, Jessica, and Mrs. V

"*B*out time you woke up, Thea. Tim's mom is gonna be here any second," Sam said. The doorbell rang, and he ran out of the bedroom.

Since it was summer vacation and Mom was working, Sam had to go to Tim's house on weekdays. I was allowed to stay home on my own, which was fine with me because I had Angela right next door.

"Don't forget your inhaler," I said loudly.

"I'm not gonna have asthma today," Sam shouted. He dashed back into the bedroom and grabbed the fat box which held his matchbox car collection.

"Sam, you have to take it with you every day."

"You're not my mother, Thea," he said, but I saw him shove the inhaler into his pocket. "See ya later, fumigator!" He ran out of the bedroom and I heard the front door slam.

I knelt on the bed and jerked the window curtain

aside. A lavender paper, like a tiny piece of laundry, was clipped to the pulley line. I slid the window open and snatched it.

Dear Thea,
Could you please meet me in the alley?
❀ *Love, Angela* ❀

Across the breezeway, I saw Angela's silhouette in her window. I gave her the thumbs-up sign, bounced off my bed, and grabbed my shorts and T-shirt off the floor. I dressed, shoved my front door key into my pocket, nabbed an apple off the kitchen table, and headed out. I liked the loud echo my thongs made as they hit the concrete steps—*slap, slap, slap.* I trotted through the courtyard to the alley behind our building.

Between the first two sets of carports, there was a low wall made of cinder blocks. I climbed onto it and sat munching my apple. I gazed up at the sky. A fat crescent moon hung in a cloudless eternity of blue.

Why can we see the moon during the daytime? Seems like we should only see it at night. I'm happy we get to live in Mamac's house! Of course it would be better if Mamac were still alive. If she could still be alive, I would be glad to stay in our apartment. But if she can't be alive, then it will be so cool to live in a real house again—especially hers. No more sharing a room with Sam. Angela is my only friend here anyway, and her family's moving— lickety-split. That Uncle Ray—he's so awful—calling Mom and being mean and hanging up on her. Oh, I miss Dad so much—and Mamac.

Angela's arrival burst my thoughts like a bubble. She was breathless from running.

"Mother would not allow me to leave. First, she insisted that I eat breakfast. Then she wanted to go over my summer wardrobe. 'You must dazzle the masses when you go out, Angela. Remember, you are special.'"

"You sound just like her. Very scary," I teased.

Angela scrambled up beside me. "Thea, would you like to go for a bike ride?"

"Sure. Where to?"

"Well, during graduation, the most gorgeous boy in all of Los Angeles, and probably the entire western hemisphere, told me he is going to start swim camp at Mar Vista Pool."

I felt a tug of dread. "Ricky? Why did he tell you that?"

"I asked him—you know, just chatting—what he was doing this summer. He said he is on the Mar Vista Marlins swim team. When he is fifteen, he is going to be a lifeguard. He is so dreamy, Thea. Would you like to go to the pool?"

"For what?"

"To see if he is there."

"Angela, why didn't you just ask him when he's going to be there?"

"That would be too forward. Besides, I do not know if he likes me, or—"

"He probably does like you, or he will soon." I couldn't imagine why any boy wouldn't like Angela.

"Do you think so?" Angela's smile was huge and annoying. "I want to bump into him by accident. He has an older brother . . . ." She batted her eyes mischievously.

"So?"

"He is a lifeguard, and he is gorgeous too. Maybe you would like him."

"I wouldn't," I said flatly.

"There will be other cute boys there—teenagers. Shall we go?"

Teenagers. Boys with muscles (at least some of them) and hairy armpits. Girls with bright, two-piece bathing suits, even bikinis. Girls with breasts and waists and hips. Another tug of dread.

"Sure. Why not?" I said.

We rode the short mile to Mar Vista Park and sailed through the parking lot to the swimming pool. At the deep end, we dismounted and pushed our bikes between the bushes and the tall chain-link fence that surrounded the pool. Kids were just arriving. A few were swimming. Most were lying or sitting on the cement pad around the pool.

"No swim camp. No lessons either. Let's ask in the office," I said.

Angela didn't answer. Her face was pressed against the fence. Her fingers grasped the rigid wire. Her eyes were fixed on something—or someone.

A patchwork of colorful towels was laid out on our side of the pool. Two girls were sunbathing. Two boys sat with their backs to us and were play-slapping each other. A boy with brown curls that fell past his ears sat on a towel. His knees were drawn up, and he hugged them with his arms. He was tan even though summer had only just begun. He was really cute. He was Ricky.

"He is here," Angela sighed. "I wish we had brought

our suits."

"Looks like he's just hanging out," I said. *I am so glad we didn't bring our suits.*

"Not her!" Angela's cheeks went splotchy red.

"Who?" I peered back at the kids by the pool—a girl in a bright red bikini was walking in our direction. Her stride screamed confidence. Jessica! The red towel spread out next to Ricky told the rest of the story. Jessica was staring at him and grinning. Ricky was watching her.

Angela dropped her hands from the fence. She took a step back and bumped her bike. It toppled, hitting my bike as it went. They landed in a tangled heap.

The falling bikes didn't make much noise, but the commotion was enough to catch Jessica's attention. She looked right at us and, in a split second, took it all in: Angela and me outside the fence, staring in at the crowd, the bikes knocked over. She didn't miss a beat. She turned her back to us and sat cross-legged next to Ricky. Then she wiggled her bottom to get closer to him and whispered in his ear. Ricky turned. He recognized Angela and waved. Jessica laughed and pointed at us.

"Look who's spying on us," she said loudly.

The other two boys stopped their roughhousing and turned to stare. The two girls rolled onto their stomachs, and I recognized Crystal and Claire. They shielded their eyes from the sun so they could stare too.

I tried to disentangle the bikes and tripped. Angela pulled her bike up and waited for me.

"Toodle-oo," Jessica called as we rode away. "Have fun, kiddies."

Angela pedaled so furiously, I could barely keep up.

Away from the pool, past the playground, she followed the concrete path that wove through the park, around the baseball fields, and up a steep hill.

I think Angela would have kept on riding, but the path ran straight into a locked gate. A tall chain-link fence topped with razor wire encircled the three radio towers that crowned the hilltop. Kids called them the Eiffel Towers. At night you could see their red lights blink from all over Mar Vista.

Angela straddled her bike and wiped her nose with the back of her hand. Her eyes were wet. "That Jessica is the most wicked creature. She hates me, and she does not even know me."

"Jessica-the-jerk," I sighed.

"Mother is friends with her mother now—bridge club, I believe."

"I didn't know that," I said. "My parents used to play bridge. But now since Dad's gone—"

"Oh, Thea. Mamac's funeral—I forgot to ask you."

I told her about the cameo brooch, our plans to move to Mamac's house, and Uncle Ray's phone call to Mom the night before.

"You are so brave. Your uncle sounds ghastly. I would be terrified."

"It's just life," I said. But that *Angela is better than me* feeling hung in the air. "You want to see the cameo when we get back? It's really cool."

"Most definitely," Angela said.

"I wish you were going to Jefferson Junior High with me."

"Father said last night that our new house will soon be

finished. First, Mother wanted two sinks in the kitchen, but Father said it would cost too much. Then she wanted two sinks in the bathroom, and Father said yes to that. Mother kept changing her mind about the colors in the living room—blue with gold, or red with black. They ended up hiring a decorator because she was calling him at work and making such a fuss."

"I wish you didn't have to move."

"But you are moving too. We will still see each other. We will always be friends."

"At least we have summer," I said.

"I might be going to Idaho to visit my grandparents."

"You're leaving?"

"Mother says she will lose her mind if she has to spend the entire summer in our apartment. We would go in August, so you and I still have practically the whole summer to have fun. I want to go to the pool when Ricky is there. We can go together."

"What about Jessica?"

"I do not believe she will be there all the time. She is not his girlfriend. I do not think she is, anyway. Look there. What is that?"

I looked west, expecting to see the blue-gray strip of the Pacific Ocean at the edge of the horizon, but the entire coastline was gone—blocked by white fog. The houses on the streets below us had disappeared too. Even the bike path we had just ridden on was misty. I could barely make out the swing set and slide across the field below us. Within seconds, the light changed from warm yellow to bright white as the fog blocked the sun. The air became cool and smelled salty.

"This is weird," I said. "The fog never comes in this far."

"I am freezing!" Angela said.

"If we leave right now, we can beat it home," I said.

We took off, but we couldn't beat the fog. It had crept around the hill and was in front of us. Within a few blocks, we were walking our bikes, and I could no longer see Angela's back tire in front of me. I was completely alone in a strange fog-world.

I didn't recognize our street until we were on it. We headed down the alley and stowed our bikes under the carport.

"Would you like to come over?" Angela asked.

"Yes. I'll get the cameo so I can show it to you."

I ran up to my apartment and retrieved the cameo from the heart-box on my dresser. When I got back downstairs, the fog was as thick as oatmeal.

Like a blind person, I walked down the alley and through the courtyard of Angela's apartment building.

"Angela?" My voice sounded muffled in the ghost-fog. Suddenly, a shape was in front of me, and I bumped right into her.

Angela screamed and grabbed my arm. We laughed.

"You okay?" I asked.

"Oh my gosh, yes. The fog is so scary."

We clambered up Angela's stairwell. It was enclosed like mine, and our steps echoed against the concrete walls. There was less fog in the stairwell, but there was still fog. When Mrs. V appeared on the landing at the top of the stairs, she looked like she was standing in the spooky mist of a movie set.

"Angela! Where have you been? I have been worrying myself into a migraine. Riding a bicycle in the fog is a perilous activity."

I slid the cameo into my back pocket so Mrs. V wouldn't see it.

"I am sorry, Mother. We were at the park. We tried to stay out of the fog, but—"

"But nothing. Thea may stay until three o'clock. Then she must return home. I told you, we have a date with the decorator. Today we select the upholstery for the settee in the foyer."

"Yes, Mother."

Mrs. V served us crustless cucumber and cream cheese sandwiches. We ate silently and watched her arrange the upholstery samples on the table. *She's dressed like she's going to a party—a cocktail party. Her high heels are cool. Is it hard to walk in them? Mrs. V makes it look easy. Does she get her hair up like that by herself? I think that's called a French bun—so smooth and blonde. Angela will dress like her when she's grown-up. That dress is really tight. Mrs. V has no fat bulges. She always wears red lipstick . . . .*

"Here are the latest swatches. I adore this copper with crimson," Mrs. V said. She placed the sample next to the other fabric squares and drummed the table top with her red fingernails.

Cool nails—they match her lipstick.

"I thought you liked the green with gold," Angela said.

"Emerald with gold is passé."

They clucked and cooed, and I stopped listening. *I miss my family—the way it was before. I want Mom home with us. I want Dad to be at work and to come home at dinnertime. I want to be back in our old house. I want Mamac to be back in her house, always happy to see me.*

After we ate, Angela and I escaped down the hall to her bedroom. I loved Angela's room: white furniture with gold edging (French Provincial, she had told me), a canopy bed with a lilac bedspread and matching bed skirt, and pillow shams with ruffled lilac edging.

We stood by the window, and I took the cameo out of my pocket and handed it to her.

"It is lovely. Where is it from?" Angela asked.

"I don't know. Mamac wore it when she dressed up. Mom said it gets passed to the oldest girl."

"The light shines through the back, like a shell," Angela said, holding it up. She handed it back to me. "Would you like to play *War*?"

"Sure," I said. I set the cameo on the nightstand so I wouldn't squish it in my pocket, and Angela got her cards from her games cupboard.

We spent the afternoon playing *War* then moved on to the board game, *Life*. We sprawled on the floor and munched grapes and Oreo cookies. We were at the end of the second round of *Life* when, suddenly, Angela's door flew open, and Mrs. V stepped into the room.

"Angela, look at the clock! It is four forty-five. I was taking my repose. We have missed our appointment."

Mrs. V held a wine glass half-full of rose-colored liquid. Her eyes swept the floor—empty Oreo bag, scattered plates with grape stems. "You have spoiled your appetite," she said.

She took a step. Her ankle wobbled, and her pointy high heeled shoe bumped the *Life* board, creating a landslide of money, cards, and cars.

"Look what you have done! If you cannot plan better, you cannot have company. Thea, it is time for you to go. Angela has things to do. She cannot be shiftless all day."

Angela started to cry. I jumped to my feet and ran out of the Vanderlins' apartment. *How is Angela supposed to keep track of Mrs. V's appointments? It wasn't our fault she fell asleep. She's so crazy!*

It was a relief to walk through my own front door—like I had escaped enemy territory. I washed the dishes and made dinner for me, Mom, and Sam: macaroni and cheese, and iceberg lettuce salad. At six o'clock, Mom arrived with Sam.

"You made dinner!" Mom exclaimed. "My most-wonderful daughter." She kissed me on the forehead.

"Macaroni and cheese! Yummy!" Sam said.

I told Mom about Mrs. V's freak-out.

"Maybe you shouldn't go over there for a while. She sounds like she's off her rocker," Mom said.

"But Angela is my best friend."

"I know, honey. But drinking wine in the middle of the day, telling you to leave—so rude!"

Mom started clearing the table, muttering, "Thinks she's better than everyone else. Just a drunk. Not so fancy after all."

I better not say any more about it. Mom might make a rule that I can't see Angela. That would be a catastrophe. She's my best friend. I have to see her.

After dinner, we sat on the couch and cuddled with

Mom. *Bewitched* was on TV—my favorite show.

When I went to bed, I said a little prayer:

Dear Mamac,
I wish you didn't have to die. I miss you so
much. I know you are in heaven now. Please tell
Dad I love him. And, Mamac, thank you for
giving me your cameo.
Amen.

Cameo? Cameo! I left my cameo at Angela's!

I got on my knees and looked out the window—no note on the line. Across the breezeway, Angela's room was dark. *I'll have to wait until tomorrow to get it.*

I settled back under my quilt. I could hear Sam's even breathing across the room. My mind slid into that shadowy, quiet place where dreaming begins. But something was different. The dream shadows were tinged with neon green. The green grew brighter until it was so bright, I had to shield my eyes with my hand, but not my real hand, my dream hand.

The neon light was all around me. Then it was behind me, and I was sinking. Sinking back into it—not my body, just my mind—slipping backward into a pool of spinning green light. Slipping, sinking, dropping back, down, deep.

Bam! Everything stopped. I was lying on a hard surface—cool air around me. I opened my eyes—mist, crooked limbs, long leaves. *The willow tree!*

In the night sky above the treetop, a swirling cloud of pink mist hovered. It looked like glowing cotton candy. The mist thinned. *There's something there—inside . . . . It's a person. A woman.* She glowed as if a light were shining right through her skin. Pink sparks shot from her gown like thousands of never-ending sparklers.

The woman stepped down as if she were descending a staircase, but there was no staircase—just air. When she reached the top of the tree, she stopped, and her eyes landed on me. *It's Mamac! She's young like in the photos Mom showed us.*

I stood up, not taking my eyes off her for even one second. "Mamac," I called, but my voice was barely a whisper.

Mamac reached her arms toward me. I tried to move, but my body was so heavy—like I was in a super-gravity zone. The light dimmed. My heart fluttered—first with panic, then with sorrow. *I'm losing her. I'm losing her—again.*

I clawed the air, but all I could grasp were the rough leaves of the tree. Mamac disappeared, then the tree blurred, and it was gone too.

When I awoke the next morning, I lay in bed staring at the ceiling and thinking about my dream. *It felt so real. I miss Mamac so much . . . .* I sat up and swung my feet onto the carpet.

Sam came in. "You're awake! Hey, what's that?" he said, pointing at the bed.

I looked down. The white bedsheet was dotted with bits of gray-green.

"I have no idea," I said. I ran my hand over the broken bits, and they jumped about. "Looks like—" I didn't finish. They were broken leaves.

I got out of bed and made Sam an English muffin. I could hardly wait for him to leave. I was already scribbling a note for Angela when there was a knock on the front door. It was Tim and his mom.

"See ya later, regurgitator!" Sam shouted as he left.

I clipped my note to the pulley and whisked it over to Angela's window. *Tap, tap, tap.* I jiggled the line to make the clothespin rap on the glass.

Meet in alley —ten minutes—Important!

❀ Thea ❀

Angela's arm shot out and snatched the note. She gave me the thumbs-up sign. I got dressed, then I toasted an English muffin for myself and gobbed margarine on it. The melting margarine dripped onto my hands, and I wiped them on my shorts. Before I grabbed my front door key, I ran back into my bedroom and brushed some of the leaf fragments off the bed sheet into my hand.

By the time I arrived in the alley, Angela was waiting.

"Thea!" she exclaimed. "I woke up holding your cameo. I had the most peculiar dream. I was in Mamac's garden. It was foggy—like yesterday. A pink light appeared above the willow tree, and this woman—"

"She stepped down an invisible staircase," I interrupted.

Angela stared at me and kept talking. "She reached for me. I wanted to go to her, but I could not move."

"Angela, we had the same dream!"

Rendezvous in a Dream

*L*ook!" I showed Angela the broken leaves. "I found these in my bed! They're from the dream."

"That is very strange," Angela said. "Maybe the leaves were already in your bed, or perhaps someone shook out a towel by your bed."

"No, Angela. That didn't happen."

"The woman was so familiar. Who can she be?"

"It was Mamac," I said.

"Mamac?"

"Yes. Mamac—but when she was young. She is trying to talk to us."

Angela stared at me. "That is not possible—"

"I've heard of people getting messages in their dreams. You know, from family who have died."

"What kind of messages?"

"I don't know. Just messages. What if Mamac wants to give us a message?"

"She did not give us a message," Angela said.

Ideas popped into my head like pieces of a puzzle fitting snugly together. "We need to find each other in the dream!"

"Find each other in the dream?" Angela asked incredulously.

"Yes! You could wear the cameo tonight when you go to sleep."

"You think if I wear your cameo when I go to sleep, I can find you in your dream?"

"Our dream."

"That is not possible, Thea. That is—I am sure Mother would not approve."

"You can pin it to your nightgown. We could try."

Angela looked away. "Come get your cameo," she said.

"What about your mother?"

"What about her?"

"I mean, is she . . ." I didn't want to say, *drunk*, so I said, "mad at me?"

"She was upset with me, not you. She is all right now. Anyway, it is still morning. She does not have wine until lunch. After you left, she lectured me for ten minutes. 'Angela, you must be more helpful to me. Angela, life is very difficult for me. Wait until you are married, then you will understand.' When Father came back from work, she acted sweet as though nothing had happened."

"Did you tell him what she did?" I asked.

"No. I could not do that. She would punish me when Father is at work if I did that. She would make me stay with her in the apartment all day."

"That would be awful."

"She is not always like this. She is going through one of her moods. That is what she calls it. She sleeps, drinks wine, and gets upset. She will be better soon—at least for a while."

"I hope so." But I couldn't help but think: *Mom is the same person every day, and I like having Sam around, even if he is a dork.*

We went up to Angela's apartment. Mrs. V was on the phone. She was pacing the living room like a caged lion, dragging the long phone cord behind her.

"I will not suffer the entire summer in this wretched place. Just a minute, Larry. Hello girls," she said with her red lipstick smile. "What are you doing?"

"Nothing," Angela said.

"Remember, we are meeting the decorator today. We still need to select the upholstery."

"Yes, Mother."

We scampered down the hall to Angela's room. I closed the door behind us.

"I feel like I am a mouse, and she is a cat waiting to pounce on me," Angela said.

"So, where's my cameo?" I said, looking around.

Angela walked over to the nightstand. "Where did it go? It was right here." She dropped to her knees and ran her fingers through the shag carpet under the bed and behind the nightstand.

"Maybe your mother took it," I said. *Mrs. V probably won't give it back,* I thought miserably.

Angela pulled back the lavender bedspread, and we searched between the sheets. "Where can it have gone?" she said.

I grabbed one of her lavender pillows—nothing underneath. I grabbed the other pillow. A flint of light shot out, hit Angela in the chest, and fell to the floor.

"Here it is!" Angela said, picking up the cameo.

"How did it get under the pillow?"

"I cannot imagine. I told you, I woke up holding it, but I left it on the nightstand. I am sure of it."

I slipped the cameo into my shorts pocket. "I'll see you later," I said.

"I will send you a note when we return from the decorator."

When I arrived home, I put the cameo back in the heart-box on my dresser. *It was a dumb idea. Meet in a dream? You can't meet someone in a dream. It would have been fun to try though. I wish she had wanted to try.*

I spent the day reading and watching TV. I was glad when Mom and Sam came home.

After dinner, Mom washed the dishes, Sam dried, and I put them away. Then I went to my room and discovered Angela's note waiting for me on the line.

Dear Thea,
  Please meet me in the alley. Bring the you-know-what.
  ❀ Love, Angela ❀

The sun had gone down, and it was almost dark. I jumped off my bed and nudged the cameo out of my heart-box with my finger. Then I went to my bedroom door and peeked out. Mom and Sam were still in the kitchen. *I won't tell Mom I'm going outside. If Sam sees me leaving, he'll want to come.*

I walked as fast and as quietly as I could through the living room, out the front door, and down the stairs, making sure my thongs didn't slap the concrete as I went. I scurried around the back of our building.

The alley was quiet. Each carport had a light in its ceiling, but it was deep inside and offered little light to the alley. I shivered. *Maybe she already left. I'll go as far as Mrs. V's Cadillac, then I'm going home.*

"Hi."

I whirled around. "You scared me," I said.

"Sorry. I was waiting by your mother's car."

Even in the dim light, I could see Angela's eyelashes were clumped and wet, and her eyes were red.

"What's wrong?" I asked.

"Nothing. Well, not nothing. I went with Mother to the decorator. Afterward, we went to *Le Bistro de Paris* for lunch. She told me something."

"What?"

"She and Father are going to play bridge tomorrow night."

"So?"

"She wants me to go with them."

"So?"

"They are going to play bridge with Jessica's parents. Mother wants me to come along and play with Jessica."

"Dang!" I said.

"I told Mother I am not friends with Jessica, but she said they are one of the few families here who are the right kind of people."

"Whatever that means," I said.

"My father knows her father through his job. Her family belongs to the country club that Mother wants to join."

I had a dad. He was the best dad in the world . . . .

Even though Angela didn't want to hang out with Jessica, I still felt jealous. Jealous that she had two parents. Jealous that she got to go out with them. Jealous that she might end up liking Jessica. Jealous that Jessica was friends with Ricky. Jealous that Ricky could end up liking Angela. I was one big blob of jealousy.

"Thea, I want to try what you said. I want to wear the cameo, and have the dream again, and look for each other under the willow."

"Why did you change your mind?"

"I am tired of so many rules. 'Angela, do what I say. Angela, you are special. Angela, you must always look your best.' I want to make my own choices. I want to be brave—like you."

"I don't think anything bad can happen. It will either work, or it won't."

"See? You are not frightened. Did you bring it?"

I opened my hand. The raised profile of the woman shone white on its amber-colored backing.

"You'll be super careful with it, right?"

"Of course," Angela said solemnly. "We can take it up to my room right now."

"What about your mother?"

"Father is home now too."

I pressed my precious cameo into Angela's palm, and we hustled up to her apartment.

The apartment air was warm and smelled like a delicious dinner had been cooked—a roast with carrots and potatoes. Mr. and Mrs. V were sitting at the dining room table. "No, Larry. I want the chandelier! It has one thousand crystals!" Mrs. V said.

"Thea forgot something," Angela said. She cupped the cameo loosely against her leg as if she weren't holding anything. Before Mrs. V could object, we scurried down the hall to Angela's bedroom.

"I will hide it here," Angela said, sliding her hand under her plump, lavender pillow. "Just so."

"How 'bout we both go to sleep at ten?" I suggested.

"Perfect." Angela led me back through the living room to the front door. "See you at the willow," she whispered.

I trotted home. By the time I walked in my front door, it was nine forty-five.

Sam was curled up with Mom on the couch, watching TV.

"Hey, where were you?" he asked, without taking his eyes from the *Felix the Cat* cartoon.

"I went to Angela's for a minute. Did I break the law or something?"

"Come sit with us," Mom invited.

I sat next to Mom and stared at the television.

"I'm tired," I said. "I'm going to bed."

"Shh," Sam said. "You're interrupting."

"Are you feeling well, hon?" Mom asked. She put her hand on my forehead. "You don't feel hot."

"Quiet!" Sam commanded.

Felix, the black-and-white cat on the TV screen, strolled along, daydreaming. Signs flashed around him. *No*

Trespassing! Scram! Stay out! But he didn't notice them.

"I'm fine," I said, pulling away from Mom.

"Going to bed early sounds like a good idea. Let's all turn in. Sam, put on your jammies."

"What the heck? It's not even night yet. What about *Felix the Cat?*"

"Felix will still be there tomorrow night. Come on, hon. Five more minutes—then lights out," Mom replied.

I was already in bed when Sam came in. "Thanks a lot, Thea," he said. "I have to go to bed now 'cause of you."

"Turn out the light," I said sternly. I turned my back to him and smiled at the wall. I was so excited—I could hardly lie still.

Sleep! I commanded myself.

I tried to see the shadows—the green glow. *You can't force it. Relax. Okay, my right foot is relaxed. Now, my left foot. My right leg is relaxed . . . .*

Up my body I went, telling each part to relax. I learned this from Dad. When I was little, he sometimes put me to bed, and if I couldn't settle down, he'd say, "Now wiggle your toes. Scrunch them up. Now let them go. Your toes are completely relaxed. Now your ankles . . ." I checked the clock on my nightstand—twenty minutes after ten. *How can we meet in our dreams if I can't fall asleep?*

I had to go to the bathroom. That really woke me up. When I got back into bed, I tried the relaxation game again. My thoughts began to wander.

I was just slipping into that cozy place between awake and asleep when the whirlpool caught me, and I was sucked backward into the spinning green light.

The air was cool. I was lying on my back on hard dirt. I

opened my eyes. The leaves of the willow tree were all around—a thousand shades of silver and black. A half-pizza moon played peek-a-boo above the tree limbs which swayed in the breeze. I stood up.

"Angela?" I called. *Behind the trunk—something white—is it . . . ?* A blonde girl in a white cotton nightgown was reclining against the willow, staring out at nothing.

"Angela," I said, ducking under a fat limb so I could stand in front of her. "How long have you been here?"

"Hello," she said in a casual tone. "I have always been here. And you?"

"Angela, it's me, Thea. You haven't always been here. This is a dream." I grabbed her bare arm and noticed Mamac's cameo pinned to the front of her nightgown. It pulsed a soft amber light.

"Thea? What are you doing here? I went to bed and— now I am here, and—oh my gosh! It worked! We are here together!" She gave me a big hug, and I nearly fell backward.

"*Shh,* Angela. Not so loud. Has Mamac come yet?"

"Mamac? Yes, Mamac. I mean, no. I mean, I do not know. I forgot to look for her."

"Remember the tree? She's supposed to appear above the tree. Why are you acting so weird?"

"Weird? Is she . . . ?"

I followed Angela's gaze to the top of the tree. "Let's go up," I said.

"But where is she? You said Mamac would be here."

"It's not like we have an appointment with her."

I went around to the front of the willow and scrambled into the crook of the massive forked branches. Angela followed. We crawled and scaled the left side—out and up. The rough bark scratched my legs through my nylon nightgown, but I didn't stop until we were just below the spot where Mamac had been the night before.

"Why is she not here?" Angela asked.

"Angela, think for a second. Even if Mamac isn't here, you and I have met in our dream and are climbing the willow tree. Isn't that cool enough?"

"I suppose. But I am freezing. I wish I had brought a sweater."

Good thing Angela couldn't see my face. I rolled my eyes, and I'm sure I looked supremely annoyed.

"Maybe we should go down," I said. "Angela? What the—why is your hair pink?" But it wasn't just Angela's hair. The branches and leaves around her were crimson, and my arms were dark red.

"Goodness gracious," Angela whispered. She was craning her neck, looking up.

I looked up too. The top of the tree was lit—as if the moon were shining a hot-pink spotlight on our willow. A mist was gathering. It was thick, like the pink whipped cream Mamac and I had once made by stirring in a drop of red food color. The whipped-cream mist churned and swirled, then the edges burned away. A woman in a gown of molten glitter appeared. She lit the air, and her auburn hair moved in phosphorescent waves.

"Mamac!" I called.

Mamac stared straight ahead as she descended an invisible staircase.

"Mamac . . ."

Her eyes fell on me, and I felt a sturdy stillness of

certainty. Like I knew something for sure, but I couldn't have explained what it was. *If I climb one more branch and inch out, I can reach her.*

But before I could try, Mamac had turned and climbed back up the invisible steps. She glanced back and smiled. Then she took a step up and vanished into the sky.

"Mamac . . ." I whispered. Disappointment fell on me like a wet blanket.

"Where did she go?" Angela said.

"How should I know?"

"Should we climb down?"

"We can't give up yet. Wait there. I'm going higher."

"Oh Thea, please be careful."

I stood up and grabbed the next branch. It was chest-high. I threw my leg over it. It shook as I struggled to get my feet under me and stand up. I grasped some wispy stems by my face to steady me as I inched forward—the soles of my bare feet reading the rough branch as I went. *We've come this far* . . . . The branch sagged under my weight. *Please don't break.*

"Wasn't she standing about here?" I said.

"A little farther out. Please take care," Angela whispered.

Like a nervous tightrope walker, I continued, stretching one arm above me and waving my hand, hoping to feel the invisible staircase. *Just stems and leaves . . .*

I withdrew my hand, and my knuckles knocked against something solid and unyielding. My heart skipped. "I found it!"

Flying

I felt along it with my fingertips. *Not round like a branch—it has angles like a cut board. It's wide—but if I stretch—I can touch both ends. It's attached—to nothing. It's floating!*

Mamac was just standing on it. If it can hold her, it can hold us. But does Mamac weigh anything? Was she really standing on it? What should I tell Angela? She'll want to climb down if she thinks it's not safe. Maybe I can grab on and . . .

On tiptoes, I grasped the back edge with both hands and transferred my weight onto my forearms. My legs were left dangling. *Can't go back now.*

I swung my leg over the top of the ledge and straddled it like a horse. After that, it was easy to turn and sit properly.

"Angela, I'm sitting where Mamac was standing—right here in the leaves! It's really strong. Come up. We can both fit." Silence. "Angela?"

Something grabbed my knee. I gasped.

"Help me," Angela pleaded.

I grabbed her by the wrist and pulled. She was half up and had got her knee down next to me, but something was holding her back.

"My nightgown is caught," she said.

I hooked my arm around her elbow, and with my free hand, I grabbed her nightie as low as I could reach and yanked it.

Rip! The gown tore. Angela was propelled forward, knocking me backward. My upper back slammed against a second hard edge which kept me from falling out of the tree.

"*Ow!* Angela, get off me!"

"I would if I could."

She was kneeling on the ledge now, but the waist of her nightgown was pulled tight under her knees. The back of her head was in my face, and she was hunched over.

She put her hand on my shoulder and shifted her weight to free her nightgown. Then she slid her bottom onto the board beside me, her ripped gown wrapped around her legs like a huge, loose bandage.

"At last," she said, sighing.

"You look like a mummy with your legs wrapped like that. Your mother would be proud of your new fashion statement."

Angela rubbed her eyes. Her hands were trembling. "Angela, you must always be a fashion leader, not a follower," she said, imitating Mrs. V. "Seeing Mamac is a formal occasion. Wear the mummy-just-got-out-of-bed gown."

We laughed like lunatics.

"Thea, I cannot believe this is happening. Are you in my dream, or am I in yours?"

"What?"

"I know I am me, so you must be in my dream," Angela said.

"I know I am me too. I told you before, it's our dream," I said firmly.

Angela looked around. "Extraordinary."

Across the yard, Mamac's roof stood black and jagged against the sky. From there, row after row of neighbor rooftops zigzagged in both directions.

"The neighborhood looks empty," Angela said.

"Everyone's gone—eaten by Godzilla."

"Do not say that, Thea. It is frightening."

"I'm kidding. Everyone is tucked in, safe and sound, asleep in their beds."

"What should we do now?"

I looked at her. The cameo was glowing like crazy. It lit her throat and chin and cast weird shadows up her face. "I think there are more steps here," I said. "My back hit one when you almost knocked me out of the tree."

Angela reached into the air behind us and found the second, invisible step. She ran her hand over it. "Follow . . . her?" she asked in a small voice.

"Yes." I tried to sound confident.

"But where did she go? If we fall," she stared into the blackness below, "the limbs will hit us all the way down. We will smash on the ground. We will probably be dead by then."

"Angela, Mamac was here. She stood right here! We're going to stand up now."

"Very well," she said doubtfully.

We squirmed until we were kneeling. Then we stood up and turned so that we were facing what we thought was the next step. "Right foot first," I said.

"Take my hand," Angela said.

I pawed the air with my foot and landed on an invisible slab of what felt like rippled, worn wood.

"Step up," I said. We cleared the tree and were standing above it. "Keep going," I commanded.

We lifted our left feet and touched the edge of the next plank. It felt firm. We stepped up.

"So far, so good," Angela said, her voice quivering.

"Again." I reached for the next board, and my foot landed squarely upon it.

Up we went. Four, five, six . . .

"That makes six. We are six steps above the tree!" Angela said.

Creeeaak. The sound came from below. The step under my feet began to vibrate.

"Angela, do you feel—"

The board began to shake.

"Earthquake?" Angela asked in a squeaky-high voice.

Like a trapdoor, the sixth step dropped—as if, suddenly, gravity *were* functioning properly. I staggered, caught myself, and somehow managed to stay on.

But Angela's hand was yanked from mine with sickening certainty. I tried to grab her, but she was out of reach. She slid off the ledge. A gasp. A groan. A scream. They bottlenecked inside my throat and escaped like the moan of a frantic, dying animal. *"Ahhnoooangelaaaaa . . ."*

Clunk. It was a sound like a gear change on an old bicycle. Then, like a super, spring-loaded diving board, the step ricocheted straight up, stopping with a jerk exactly where it had started. But I kept going—catapulted high into the air.

This was a terrible idea. I'm going to fall now . . . .
But I didn't fall.

"Thea!"

"Angela!"

Angela bobbed up beside me, her torn nightie trailing behind her like the tail of a kite.

We were as light as dandelion seeds floating above the tree. I grabbed Angela's hand, and the pillowy air encouraged us to stretch out our arms and legs. As if this were the signal to go, we glided forward.

"Thea, we are flying!"

"No kidding!" I laughed.

A gust of air swept us along, just above the treetops. Below us spread a patchwork of backyards cut into neat squares by wood fences. A few were dimly lit and scattered with patio furniture, swing sets, and an occasional swimming pool.

Above us, the sky was an infinite, luminous sapphire. The fat half-moon shone white in the east over downtown Los Angeles.

"Thea, all of Mar Vista is here," Angela said.

"This is so cool! Hey, want to check out our apartments?"

"Very well, but we better stay over back gardens. Even if this is a dream, we do not want anyone to see us."

We pointed our bodies south, toward home, and picked up speed. Moving through the air was like cutting through the deliciously cool water of a swimming pool. We were a few houses from National Boulevard when I grabbed on to the branch of a sycamore tree. I was still holding Angela's hand, and she was yanked to a stop in front of me.

"We have to cross National," I said, watching the car headlights moving in front of us. Their engines whirred as they zoomed by. We hovered and waited. It took three red lights before the street was empty. "Now!" I said. Like arrows, we shot across the wide boulevard and were off again.

"Look," I said, pointing. "Our apartments! They look different from up here—kind of small."

"Oh my goodness! My bedroom window!" Angela said.

We waved our arms and bent our knees so we could hover above the alley behind our apartment buildings.

"Should we peek in my window? Maybe I am asleep in my bed," Angela said.

"We could—but I don't think we can get right up to the window and stay there. We might break it by accident. Besides, it's too much like the *Twilight Zone*. If you see yourself asleep, you might have a feedback-loop identity crisis and never wake up."

"Goodness gracious, Thea! Another extremely frightening thought. Now I do not want to try."

I looked around. In the distance, red lights blinked from the Eiffel Towers on the hilltop above Mar Vista Park. "Let's head for the park," I said.

"I am not allowed to go to the park at night," Angela

replied.

"Are you kidding? We're not allowed to go anywhere at night, but here we are. Come on!"

I twisted and turned then locked my knees straight. We sliced the air, heading for the silhouetted hill with the blinking red lights. I felt Angela's hand in mine—warm and strong. *I'm not pulling her. She is really brave.* Parked cars speckled the streets below, but there was no one around—just block after block of unlit houses and scattered spots of light from street lamps and porch bulbs.

We entered the airspace over the park. It was pitch black except for a light at one end of the parking lot and another in front of the swimming pool office. We skimmed the treetops, and I slapped the leaves. Cold air engulfed us when we crossed the baseball fields. Up the hill, at the far end of the park, the red lights of the radio towers blinked cheerfully.

"To the towers," I said.

We sped up the hill. The chain-link fence topped with razor wire was just ahead.

"It is extremely dark here," Angela said. "Maybe we should go back."

"We will in a minute," I said. "Let's circle around so we can get higher and land on the middle tower."

We spiraled upward, then cut straight through the air, picking up speed. The middle tower loomed in front of us.

"Too fast!" Angela screamed. We bent our knees and flapped our arms. That helped a little—but not enough.

Right before we were about to crash, I threw my leg over the bar in front of me. The rough, cold metal pushed my nightgown up and scraped the back of my thigh.

Another bar, higher up, hit me in the chest. I grabbed it and hung on.

Somehow, Angela had landed with both legs over the lower bar. She looked like a rag doll with her arms and legs dangling inward.

"You okay?" I asked.

"It would seem so," she said faintly.

Off in the distance, a curve of streetlights ran along the Pacific Coast Highway. Beyond the lights, laid the infinite black of the Pacific Ocean. Behind me were the Santa Monica and San Diego Freeways. The Santa Monica Freeway went east and west, and the San Diego Freeway went north and south. They looked like two snakes forming a cross where they intersected. The snake that was the Santa Monica Freeway lifted its belly slightly so that the San Diego Freeway could pass underneath. Each freeway had a white stripe of car headlights going one way and a red stripe of taillights going the other.

"Do those people stay up all night?" I wondered out loud.

"Father says that is what makes Los Angeles a stimulating place to live. There is always something happening," Angela said.

The long tatters of Angela's nightgown flapped in the breeze that washed over us, but I wasn't cold.

"Angela," I said. "This is the best dream I've ever had."

"It is very late. We should go back to our beds."

"Okay, but how do we get there? Can we just wake up and be there?"

"Here, I will shake you. That will wake you up." Angela grabbed my shoulder and shook me.

"I'm still here."

"Here, pinch me," she said, offering her arm.

"Gladly." I pinched her hard.

"*Ow!* Stop it. That hurts."

"Weird," I said. "Okay, no biggie. We'll fly back to the willow."

"Good idea. That is the way we came. Wait. How do you know we can still fly? We could jump and fall."

"Don't say that. You might make it happen." Angela's face was almost as white as her nightgown. I checked Mamac's cameo. It was still glowing; its gold trim glinted in the moonlight. "We won't fall. This can't end with us crashing on the ground. I'll go first if you want."

"Very well," Angela said doubtfully.

"One, two, three . . ." I bent my knees and leapt. The air supported me like the softest feather pillow. "Come on." I reached for Angela and pulled her forward.

She stepped off the bar and was weightless. We stretched out horizontally to the ground and were off again, soaring like birds through the park.

At National Boulevard there were no cars, so we crossed right away. Three more blocks and the willow was easy to spot. From above, it looked like a huge shaggy head of hair.

We coasted in, still holding hands. With our free hands, we reached below us, searching for the top step of the invisible staircase.

"It was more to the left," Angela said.

We doubled back. Even though I was searching for the top step, it was startling when my hand hit its hard, invisible edge.

We grabbed on with both hands and set our feet down, but the spring action that had ejected us before kept trying to toss us back into the air. We had to fight to stay on and ended up in a handstand with our nightgowns draped over our heads! We hung on until the propelling energy subsided, then we gently planted our feet onto the bobbing ledge. Gingerly, we crawled backward down the steps to the top limb of the willow. Then we shimmied down its branches and jumped to the ground.

We were back on earth. Wet dichondra squeezed between my toes, making my feet cold.

"Thea, I don't think we are dreaming anymore," Angela said in a frightened whisper.

"Don't worry," I said. "If we're awake, which I think we are, we can run home. That's all. No big deal."

"This was an insane, bad idea. Mother is going to kill me." Angela started to cry.

I put my arm around her. "In an emergency, always stay calm," I said, trying to sound like our teacher, Mrs. Fisher.

"Is this a fire drill?" Angela asked. We burst into laughter and our worries evaporated. "You are right, Thea. Of course we can run home from here."

The yard was dark, but the driveway was darker. I ran my fingers along the rough stucco of the house to guide me. We found the gate and raced to the sidewalk. Angela's gown was ripped almost all the way around, just above the knee. She held the shredded train with one hand as we ran.

We had gone three blocks when the bright headlights of a car turned the corner and headed straight toward us. We dropped to our knees on the grass strip by the curb and hid behind a parked car. We waited until the car was two blocks away, then we jumped up and started running again. My bare feet pounded the cold, rough pavement.

National Boulevard was empty. The traffic light was red. We crossed anyway. Three more blocks and we arrived at the alley entrance behind our buildings. I grabbed Angela's arm. "How are we going to get inside?"

"There is a key to my apartment hidden above the porch light," she said.

"We don't have a key hidden," I said. "What am I going to do?"

"You better come up with me."

Our bare feet made no noise as we tiptoed up the concrete stairs to the Vanderlins' front door. The porch light was on, and Angela retrieved the key from the back of its metal rim. The lock clicked, and the door silently swung open.

The shag carpet felt wonderful under my chilly, sore feet. We tiptoed past Mr. and Mrs. V's shut bedroom door. In Angela's bedroom, the clock on her nightstand lit the time: three minutes before one o'clock.

"If we wake Sam, he can let me in," I whispered.

"But he will ask questions and will tell on us."

"Do you have a better idea?" I asked.

"How would we wake him?"

"Jiggle the pulley to make the clothespin hit the window. The tapping will wake him up. First, we'll write a note that says, *Open the front door for Thea.*"

"Well, you cannot stay here. We could never explain that."

Angela wrote the note, and we sent it over on the

pulley. I jerked the line to make the clothespin tap my bedroom window.

Nothing happened.

"Do it again," Angela whispered.

I tried again. The clothespin danced and spun in a circle as it tickled the window. We waited. The bedroom window remained dark, but the window to the left lit up.

"What room is that?" Angela asked.

"It's the bathroom," I said. "Come on, Sam. Go back to the bedroom, and open the window." Finally, the bathroom window went dark.

"Try again," Angela said.

I jerked the line. Suddenly, the window slid open, and a small hand snatched the note. The light went on in the bedroom.

Angela unpinned the cameo from her nightgown.

"Here," she whispered. "Best not forget this."

The cameo had stopped glowing. *Looks like an ordinary piece of jewelry,* I thought as I crept through the Vanderlins' living room. I hurried down the stairs, across the alley, and up to my own apartment. Sam was standing in the doorway.

"What the heck you doing out there?"

"I was locked out by accident," I whispered.

I brushed past him and headed for our bedroom, stepping as lightly as I could past Mom's bedroom door. I turned out the light and slipped the cameo into the heart-box, then I collapsed into bed. Sam had climbed back into his bed and didn't ask any more questions—at least not that night.

*T*he next morning, I was just waking up—stretching and feeling comfy under the covers—when a flood of images from the previous night bombarded my brain. My eyes flew open. *What time is it?* I looked at the clock on my nightstand: nine thirty. *Thursday morning. Mom has already left for work, and Tim's mom will be here soon to pick Sam up. I have the whole day to think about last night.*

I relaxed into my pillow. Then I looked across the room. Sam was sitting on his bed, fully dressed, staring at me.

"What were you doing at Angela's last night?"

The Plan

*W*hat?"

"How come you were at Angela's when everybody was asleep?"

"I was—I woke up, and I was outside. The door was locked. I was sleepwalking."

"Walking in your sleep? That's kind of dumb."

"It doesn't matter what you think. Just don't fink on me. Mom has enough to worry about without a dork like you making trouble."

The doorbell rang. Sam ran out of the bedroom. "See ya later aviator!" he shouted.

Alone at last. I scrawled a note and scooted it over on the pulley.

11:00 carport roof.

❀ Thea ❀

At ten fifty-five, I headed downstairs, walked to the back of my building, and crossed the alley. A dumpster stood at the far end of the carport. I climbed the metal ladder rungs built into one end and pulled myself up onto the carport roof.

The roof was flat and extended the width of twenty parking spaces. I sat in the center, cross-legged, and leaned back on my arms. Puffy white clouds dotted the sky like scattered cotton balls. The sunshine warmed my face. *It will be hot later.* I gazed at the airspace just above my building. *That's where we were last night. I can hardly believe it. Us, up in the sky, in the middle of the night!*

"Hi."

Angela's head and shoulders had appeared above the carport roof. She placed her knee on the edge of the asphalt roofing and climbed up. "This always hurts my knee," she muttered. "Is everything all right?" she asked as she sat cross-legged in front of me.

"Yes. Mom didn't wake up, and Sam hasn't said anything to her. I told him I was sleepwalking. Lame, I know. How 'bout you?"

"Fine. I threw my ripped nightgown in the dumpster. I had to smuggle it out of the house. Thea, I am frightened. What happened to us? Did we really fly, or was that part of the dream? And how did we end up wide awake in Mamac's backyard?"

"I don't know, but there's one thing I do know. Mamac is part of this. I've been thinking—we need to investigate. I have an idea."

"What? No! We should stop. We are lucky nothing bad happened to us last night."

"Don't poop out on me now! We've got to find out more. We can't let Mamac down."

"Let Mamac down? Mamac is—"

"I know, Angela. I know she's dead. But you saw her too. She was there."

"Yes, but that must have been part of the dream."

"That's what we have to find out."

"Do you want to meet at the tree again when we are asleep, or dreaming, or whatever that was?" Angela asked warily.

"Maybe we don't have to be asleep," I said.

"What do you mean?"

"If we go to the tree when we're awake, the staircase might be there. You could sleep over. We could sneak out late at night, climb the tree, and maybe find the staircase—when we *know* we are awake."

"I have to go with my parents tonight, remember?"

With everything that had happened, I had forgotten about Jessica-the-jerk. Jealousy tugged at me, but it wasn't as bad as before. Seeing Mamac and flying had been so wonderful. It made Jessica seem far away and not very important.

"How about tomorrow night? Tomorrow is Friday. Ask your mom if you can sleep over," I said.

"We cannot have another misadventure like last night. My feet hurt from running barefoot on the concrete, and if Mother discovers my nightgown is missing, she will conduct a grand inquisition."

"We'll wear shoes and bring my front door key. We'll plan the whole thing," I said.

"Like super-sleuths?" Angela asked.

"James Bond Teeny Bopper Special Agents," I said, laughing.

"The Nancy Drew Dynamos!" Angela exclaimed, clapping her hands.

"Pink Panther Dream Investigators and Tree Climbing Masters!" I hollered.

"We will have to be one of those because if we are caught, I will be dead. Killed by Mrs. Doomsday."

"Then you'll go with me?"

Angela gave me her special look. The one that meant, *you can count on me,* and I felt like the most beloved best friend in the history of the universe.

"Yes, I will go with you," she said solemnly. "Thea, we must swear an oath of secrecy."

"You're right. We should swear that we'll never tell about Mamac, the cameo, or the dream," I said.

"I swear. You know you can trust me," Angela said.

"Cross your heart and hope to die?" I asked.

"Cross my heart and hope to die." Angela crossed her heart with her index finger, then she turned her palm out, demonstrating her oath. "Now, you."

"Cross my heart and hope to die," I said, crossing my heart and offering my palm.

I felt so happy, I could have done cartwheels right across the roof. "I'll ask my mom tonight if you can sleep over," I said.

"Mother said she would take us to Mar Vista Pool today if we would like. It would be a good distraction," Angela suggested.

"Sure," I said. *How can she want a distraction from the greatest adventure ever?* Then I remembered. "Is you-know-who going to be there?"

"I hope so." Angela covered her mouth to hide her giggle.

*A*t noon, we climbed into Mrs. V's white Cadillac. I wore my old two-piece bathing suit. It was green with faded-blue flowers. The top had two buttons—front and center. They served no purpose whatsoever. I didn't even know where the suit had come from. I didn't remember buying it. I felt so chubby. When I sat, my stomach made rolls across my midsection.

Angela looked like a kid-model in her purple-and-green paisley two-piece. She carried a beach towel with purple paisley splashed across it, and she wore a thin gold chain around her left ankle.

Mrs. V wore a leopard-print one-piece. It was backless. At the pool, she positioned her chaise longue perpendicular to the sun so she could tan straight on—no shadows. Then she laid out her leopard-print towel and arranged herself on it—her ankles tipped forward, just so. Her sunglasses were huge and so dark, I couldn't tell where she was looking. *She's so elegant—so beautiful.*

Mrs. V lovingly greased her body with the gel she squeezed from a tube of *Bain de Soleil.* It made her skin orange and greasy, but it smelled wonderful—like musk and orange blossoms.

Angela and I laid our towels on the hot cement. Angela kept glancing around the pool. *She's looking for Ricky.*

We were about to sit when the three-headed monster appeared. Jessica, flanked by Crystal and Claire, were on the march and heading our way. They halted in front of us.

"You may sit with us if you'd like," Jessica said. "Just you, Angela," she added, not looking at me. Crystal and Claire stifled snickers and stared at Angela as if I didn't exist.

"Thank you, but I am here with Thea and Mother. Maybe next time."

Why is she so polite to them? My face was burning with resentment.

"Suit yourself," Jessica said. "See you tonight," she added sweetly.

As they walked away, Crystal and Claire leaned in and whispered to Jessica. Jessica threw her head back and laughed loudly. They promenaded back to their towels, Jessica's ponytail wagging defiantly.

"Evil brat," I said. Even though I detested Jessica and would never want to sit with her, I couldn't keep the jealousy beast from growling inside me.

"Oh, Thea," Angela sighed. "Look who they are with."

Across the pool, Jessica, Crystal, and Claire were sitting with Ricky and his two friends.

Angela and I had fun swimming and sunbathing that day, but Angela kept glancing at the group across the pool.

She would rather be with them. I felt like I was back in the fog, and Angela was in the sunshine. She was golden —wanted. I was hidden—unseen.

*T*hat evening, Mom made spaghetti. She didn't cook much, but her spaghetti was scrumptious—thick and meaty—perfectly satisfying in big pasta mouthfuls.

"Yummy," I said, winding spaghetti onto my fork with the help of a soupspoon. "Can Angela sleep over tomorrow night?"

Sam, who had been concentrating on trying to wind his spaghetti onto his fork as expertly as I did, stopped, sat up straight, and stared at me with unblinking, brown eyes.

"Let's see, tomorrow night is Friday. That should be fine, Thea. Any special plans?"

"No," I said. "We'll just hang out here."

"Fine, honey, but you need to clean up your room. It's getting wild in there."

"Yeah, Thea," Sam said. "It's all your mess too."

"Sure, Mom. No problem," I said, ignoring Sam. Mom stared at me, surprised at my cooperativeness. But how could I mind cleaning my room when I was going to search for an invisible staircase? Just thinking about it sent quivers of excitement through me.

After dinner, I went into Mom's bedroom to call Angela on the telephone. We didn't always use the pulley outside our windows to communicate. That was for short messages.

"Hi, Angela," I said. "Mom says you can sleep over tomorrow night. Did you ask your mother?"

"Yes. She said it would be all right. I think she is going with Father to a show. She sounded happy that I had somewhere to go." She laughed, but it wasn't a happy laugh. "Thea, I have been thinking. Please do not worry. I will not abandon you. We are in this together."

"I'm so glad, Angela. I wouldn't want to go without you."

"We are the Teeny Bopper Special Agents," Angela said, giggling.

"I was thinking we should go at midnight. That's the

earliest we can be sure that Mom and Sam are asleep."

"Good. There will not be many people out that late. I will wear my blue jeans and navy-blue sweatshirt."

"How about come at six and have dinner with us?" I said.

"Very well. What?"

"I said, is that what you are wearing?" It was Mrs. V.

"No, Mother. I have not changed yet."

"Hang up the phone. Who are you talking to?"

"I am talking to Thea about sleeping over tomorrow night. Thea, I have to go."

Angela hung up, and I was about to do the same when I heard, *click.*

Weird. Was someone listening on the other phone?

I hung up the receiver and ran to the kitchen. The yellow wall phone by the stove was hung up, but its coiled cord was swaying slightly. Sam was a few feet away, getting a popsicle out of the freezer.

"Want one?" he asked.

I studied his face. *Was he listening on the phone? If I say I know he was listening, he might admit it and start asking questions again about last night. Or worse—he might tell Mom.*

"No thanks," I said. I turned and left the kitchen.

Three to the Tree

*T*he next day, Angela went clothes shopping with her mother. I did my laundry and cleaned up my side of my bedroom like Mom asked. Angela came over at six o'clock with her sleeping bag and overnight things. Mom picked up a pizza, and the four of us sat at the kitchen table and ate. That is, Sam and Mom ate. Angela and I picked.

"Aren't you girls hungry?" Mom asked.

"I apologize, Mrs. MacRobert. The pizza is very delicious, but I ate lunch in Beverly Hills with Mother, and I do not have much of an appetite," Angela said.

"What's your excuse, Thea?" Sam asked.

"What's it to you?" I said. "Mom, can we be excused?"

"Sure," Mom said, looking confused.

Angela and I went to my bedroom and shut the door. We arranged our sleeping bags side by side on the floor like we always did when she slept over.

Angela sat down cross-legged on her bag. "My

stomach is in knots," she said.

"Mine too," I said, kneeling on my bag.

"Your brother is a pest."

"Tell me about it. I have to live with him. I even have to share a room with him. So, what happened at Jessica's last night?"

"We had a nice time. Jessica said she was sorry she laughed when my bike fell over that day at the pool."

"She didn't just laugh. She said, 'Look who's spying on us,'" I reminded her.

"She promised that she is not going steady with Ricky. They are just friends. She is going to set us up."

"How?"

"She is going to ask him if he likes me." Angela's face lit up like a Christmas tree when she said this.

"She's a jerk," I said.

"Her bedroom is cool. She has a beanbag chair and a stereo record player."

"Groovy," I said glumly.

"What shall we do this evening?"

"Want to watch TV?"

"Perfect. That will not look suspicious."

Sam was already watching *Star Trek* in the living room. We lay on the floor in front of the couch and watched too.

Angela kept fidgeting and asking, "What time is it?"

"Why do you keep asking that? Got a date?" Sam asked.

"I was just wondering," Angela replied.

"Sam, what's your problem?" I said.

"Your ugly face," Sam said.

"Shut up!" I said.

"Mommy! Thea told me to shut up."

And that's how the evening went—until finally, it was ten o'clock.

"Angela, let's go to bed," I said.

"Grand idea," she said, jumping to her feet.

"Good night, Mom," I said.

"Good night, girls. Sweet dreams. Sam, time to get your bed made up on the couch."

Angela and I put on our nightgowns, turned out the light, and wiggled into our sleeping bags.

"We should try to sleep a little," I whispered.

"My stomach hurts. I do not think I will fall asleep. But just in case, should we set your alarm?"

"No, it's too loud. Don't worry. I'll wake up at the right time. I've always been able to wake up at the exact time I set in my head."

I closed my eyes but couldn't get comfortable. My nightgown was twisted around my legs, and I felt hot. I dozed and dreamt I was running down an unlit street somewhere in Mar Vista, searching for the willow tree. It appeared far away, and I ran toward it, but when I got close, the branches were going the wrong way. The dream repeated with different streets and different willows until I awoke with a start. I checked the clock: exactly midnight.

Angela was curled up on her side. I put my hand on her shoulder, and her eyes popped open.

"Time to go," I whispered.

We dressed in silence. I put my front door key in my pocket, and we crept down the hall—past Mom's door, and into the living room.

I stopped in front of the couch and checked Sam. His eyes were closed, and his breathing sounded deep and regular. *Good. He's asleep.*

I opened the front door, and we tiptoed down the stairs and into the alley behind the building. The carport lights were off, and it was a secret world back there—dark and still. I glanced around at the deep recesses of the carports. They were black holes where anything might be hiding.

We linked arms tightly and walked in sync, taking big, hurried steps to the sidewalk. We turned right.

"Two more blocks and we'll be at National," I said breathlessly.

"Precisely so," Angela said.

She looked over her shoulder for the umpteenth time. *She sure is nervous.* "No one—" I was going to say, *is around,* but suddenly, Angela grabbed my forearm and dug her nails into me. *"Ouch!"* I cried.

"Thea, there is someone back there," she whispered fiercely.

"What?" I looked over my shoulder. At the end of the block, I saw a dark figure.

We started walking super fast. When we got to the corner, we made a quick left. Then we started running.

"What should we do?" Angela said.

Up ahead, a thick laurel hedge ran along a driveway between two houses.

"There," I said, running toward it. I dove behind the hedge, pulling Angela with me.

Seconds passed. Quick steps scuffed the sidewalk. They were getting louder. My heart pounded.

A figure ran past. The light of the streetlamp revealed who it was.

"Sam!" I exclaimed.

Sam froze, then looked in every direction, trying to figure out where the voice had come from. I stood up.

"Sam!" I repeated.

Sam trotted over to us. His eyes sparkled with excitement, and his hair was spiky like he had just rolled out of bed. He was wearing the brown terrycloth robe and matching slippers Mamac had given him last Christmas. He looked as cuddly as a big brown teddy bear, and part of me wanted to give him a hug and not be mad at him. But I shoved aside these tender thoughts and demanded, "What are you doing, running around out here in your bathrobe? Are you crazy?"

"Where are you going? Two nights ago you were at Angela's when everybody was asleep. You're not allowed to do that. Tonight, I want to come too."

"Good grief, Samuel," Angela said. "It is illogical to say, 'You are not allowed to do that, so I want to come too.'"

"You're not allowed to go out in the dark without Mommy, and I want to know where you're going. I want to come."

"Wait there," I commanded. Angela and I moved a few feet away for a private conference.

"What shall we do?" Angela asked.

"I think he's been planning to follow us since he listened on the phone last night."

"He listened on the phone? You did not tell me that."

"I wasn't sure. I thought I heard someone hang up

after you. It doesn't matter now. We've got to take him with us. If we don't, he'll tell on us for sure."

"But if we let him come, he will have so much more to tell!" Angela replied. "He cannot keep a secret."

"I can't make him walk back alone. If we take him home, we'll have to stay there with him. The invisible staircase probably isn't going to be there anyway. Let's let him come. Okay?"

"I suppose he must join us," Angela said.

"Hopefully, he won't wreck everything," I muttered.

We walked back to Sam. "All right, you can come," I said. "But you have to swear you won't tell anyone about this. And, we're not telling you what we're doing until we get there."

"I won't tell. I swear," Sam said.

We backtracked to the corner then walked the block to National Boulevard.

"Let's not wait on the street corner," I said. "If we stay back here, where these apartments are, anyone who drives by won't see us. Then, when the coast is clear, we'll run across, even if the light is red."

"Cross when the light is red? We can't cross when—"

"Sam, shut up!" I said.

One car passed and then another. We edged toward the corner. More headlights, but they were down at Sawtelle Boulevard. Our light was green.

"Let's go," I said, pulling Sam and Angela with me.

We ran across National, then we half-walked, half-ran the remaining three blocks to Monroe Street.

"Mamac's house!" Sam said. "We're not allowed over here until we move in."

"Be quiet. We're not going *in* the house," I said. We headed down the driveway. I opened the gate and shut it behind us. We were swallowed by darkness.

"Let's hold hands," I said.

"Okay," Sam said. His voice sounded small and afraid.

We crept along until we reached the back of the house. I touched the rough stuccoed corner. *Right inside this wall —my bed, Mamac's sewing machine . . . Don't think about that now!*

At the head of the brick path, it was more open. A fat moon, nearly full, scattered patches of light between the dark shadows. The yard was vast and unfamiliar. In the distance, the silhouette of the great willow tree was black against the night sky.

"I changed my mind. I want to go home," Sam said.

"Look, Sam," I whispered. "You wanted to come, so now you're here. But if you're scared, we can forget it. Angela and I will take you home. It's no big deal. We'll come back without you."

Sam stiffened. "No. I wanna come too. I'm not scared, but what are we doing here?"

"We have to check something in the tree," I said.

"What tree?"

"Good grief! The willow tree!" Angela said.

"That's all we can tell you right now," I said. "Are you coming, or not?"

"Yes, I'm coming," Sam said solemnly.

The brick path was not wide enough for the three of us, so we walked single file.

"I'll lead," I said.

"I am next," Angela said.

"Hey, I'm not going last. It's dark back here. I don't wanna go last."

"Angela, will you please let him go in the middle?" I said.

"Fine, but I am not going last up the tree," she declared.

I led the way down the brick path and across the dichondra. *Will Mamac appear?* I wondered as I pushed aside the willow's shaggy veil of leaves and entered the sheltered circle. I looked up but saw only twisted branches against the indigo sky. A gentle breeze moved through the yard, and the leaves made a rustling-rattling sound.

"Sam should wait here while you and I go up," I said.

"Excellent idea," Angela said.

"No way, Thea. I'm not staying here by myself!"

"We'll just be gone a few minutes," I said. "It'll be too hard for you to climb in your robe and slippers."

"I can climb this tree as good as you. I'm not staying here!"

"All right. But you better be careful," I said.

"I am going after Thea. You will have to go last," Angela said.

"Okay, I'll go last. Don't have a cow."

I laid my hands in the crook of the trunk and hopped into the tree. Angela followed. Sam made a running jump, and Angela and I grabbed him from above as he scrambled up. We inched our way up the big branch on the left. *This is a lot easier in jeans and tennis shoes than it was barefoot and wearing my nightgown.*

When we reached the third level of branches, the limb supporting us drooped as if it might snap off.

"We're too heavy," I whispered. "Wait here. I'll go first, then you guys can come." I looked down. The blackness had swallowed everything—no tree limbs, no solid earth. A wave of jitters swept through me. *This is nuts. I could fall and break my neck! But we're here. This was our plan. We've got to keep going.*

I climbed onto the next branch—right below where the invisible staircase had been two nights before. I stood up and placed one foot in front of the other, grasping skinny branches by my face for balance.

I raised one arm and swept my fingers through the air above me. Nothing. I inched along and reached again, wiggling my fingers.

"What's Thea doing up there?" It was Sam's voice.

My arm was so tired from holding it above my head that I had to switch arms.

One last try. I raised my hand and—*ouch!* I hit something hard. I ran my fingers along it. *Long and flat. Thick as a bench. Corners.* My heart hammered.

"It's still here!"

Fire!

I reached across and grabbed its back edge with both hands. Then I swung my leg sideways and pulled myself up. I got my knees under me, twisted, and sat.

I peered into the darkness where my companions were waiting. "Come on," I whispered.

In a few seconds, Angela bumped my dangling feet. "There's room for you right here," I said, patting the spot next to me. "Go out a few more inches."

"As you say," she said uncertainly. She inched out, then turned and reached for the ledge.

"Jump," I said.

I grabbed the back of her sweatshirt between her shoulder blades and pulled as Angela swung her foot up and rolled herself across my lap. She positioned her knees on the ledge and sat.

"Come on, Sam. You can squeeze in between us," I whispered.

"I can't reach you," he whined.

"Where are you?" I said.

"Right here."

On the limb below, by the tree trunk, I could just make out his bulky shape.

"Sam, you need to hold on to a branch and walk out to us. One foot in front of the other," I said.

Silence.

"If you stay there, the boogeyman will eat you," Angela said.

There was a rustling sound, and something grabbed my calves. I jumped.

"*Ahrhrhrhaaa!*" It was Sam. "Thea, help me!" His voice was muffled because his face was smushed against my jeans.

"Sam, what are you doing? Angela, why did you tell him that?"

"I thought it would help him move along," she said.

"You're hilarious. He's strangling my legs. How is he going to reach the ledge?"

"We can pull him up."

"Sam?"

No answer.

"Sam! Answer me, or we're leaving you there."

"No, don't leave me. The boogeyman will eat me."

"I'm going to pull you up with my legs. Then we're going to grab you. You need to help."

I tried to straighten my knees to lift him, but Sam was heavy.

"Grab him, Angela! Sam, climb. Dang it! Let go of my legs and climb!"

Angela took hold of one arm, and I got the other. We pulled, grabbed, and rolled him. Sam ended up lying facedown across our laps.

"Put your knee here," Angela said.

Sam got his knees on the ledge between us and squeezed a seat for himself.

"You okay?" I asked.

"Super duper," he said unhappily.

I put my arm around him. "You're fine, Sam."

"Can you believe it?" Angela said. "It is still here!"

"It's a miracle," I said.

"What is this? Some kinda tree house you guys built?" Sam asked.

"Not exactly," Angela said. "Your sister can explain it."

"This may sound totally wacky, Sam, but Mamac led us here. It's not a tree house. It's an invisible staircase."

"Mamac? In—divisible staircase?"

"Invisible," Angela corrected.

"That means you can't see it," I said.

"I know what it means," Sam said. He touched the ledge under him as if touching it could tell him whether or not he could see it.

"Maybe it was too dark to tell when you climbed up, but this ledge is invisible," I said.

I told Sam about the dream Angela and I had shared. I think being eight helped him believe the impossible was possible. After all, he believed in Santa Claus and the tooth fairy. Why not this?

When I got to the part about crashing into the Eiffel Tower, he said, "Cool! I wanna go there!" and began swinging his legs and squirming in his seat.

"Hold still!" Angela hissed.

"We haven't decided where to go. Angela, do you think we should wait for Mamac?"

"Mamac died," Sam said.

"Yes, I know she died. But I told you, she was here. We saw her."

"Sometimes when you're dreaming, you can see people who have died. Mommy told me that," Sam said matter-of-factly.

"What are you talking about?" I asked.

"I see Daddy sometimes—in my dreams. Mommy said it's not really Daddy. I'm just memoring him."

"Oh my gosh," Angela said under her breath. "You mean, *remembering. Memoring* is not a word."

He's right, I thought. *It was just a dream. Mamac isn't going to appear now. She can't.* We sat there for a moment, not talking. I broke the silence, "Angela, should we go up?"

Angela stared at me over the top of Sam's head. The moonlight illuminated the fear in her big blue eyes. "Yes?" she said.

"Let's find out if the rest of the staircase is here, and if it is, we'll climb it—just like we planned," I said, trying to sound confident.

"So we can fly!" Sam chimed in.

I reached back and swooped the air behind us. *Bam!* I hit the second step. "It's here," I said.

Sam turned and reached up to touch it. "Wow. It is in—visible . . . ."

Angela and I knelt, then stood up. Then Sam stood, squeezing between us. We turned in unison so that we were facing the staircase.

"Hold hands," I said. "Now raise your right foot."

"She said *right*," Angela whispered. I felt Sam switch feet.

The second step held steady as we stepped into the cool air above the tree.

"Left foot," Angela said.

We raised our left feet and stepped up. And so we made our way, balancing, and saying, "Right, left, right, left . . ."

When we climbed the sixth stair, it felt solid too.

"Isn't this the sixth?" Angela asked.

I felt a slight vibration through my shoes. "Sam, I should warn you—"

Suddenly, the sixth step dropped. Angela gasped. I slid forward and almost lost my balance. *Creak-clunk!* The step jerked to a stop then rebounded with a jolt, hurling us into the air.

I was facedown. Angela was upside down, and since we were still holding hands, Sam was twisted somewhere in-between. Angela kicked the air and worked her feet so that she was facedown too. That straightened Sam. I reached for Angela's free hand, and we formed a circle— like three parachutists free-falling, except instead of falling, we floated.

"Wow!" I huffed. "That last step is rough."

"This is great! Let's go to the Eiffel Towers!" Sam shouted.

"*Shh.* Not so loud, Samuel," Angela whispered. "What do you think, Thea? Should we?"

"We've already done that. Let's do something

different," I said. "Like . . . go to our school."

"You mean, Mar Vista Elementary?" she said. "It is not really our school anymore since we graduated."

"I mean our old school," I said.

"Very well, but tonight we are not dreaming. If someone sees us, they will—I do not know what they will do, but it will not be good, and we will be in trouble, and our secret will be ruined," Angela said.

"No kidding. We'll fly over backyards as much as we can," I said. Angela and I let go of each other's hands, but we still held hands with Sam so that he remained between us. "Are you ready, Sam?" I asked.

"*¡Vámonos!*" Sam started tugging, and Angela and I slid forward and banged heads.

"Ouch! Stop that!" Angela scolded.

"Sorry."

Angela and I used our free arms to coax the air, and we spread out again. "Kick your feet," I ordered Sam.

We turned east and began to glide, but we were out of sync with each other and flew at different levels and speeds which made our arms either stretch out painfully or crumple as we collided and bumped each other. We passed over Mamac's backyard and then over her roof. Like an overloaded barge, we wobbled across the street to the block that ran perpendicular to Monroe Street.

The school was less than a mile away, but it seemed to take forever to get there. We had to make a two-block detour to avoid Hughes Market, the twenty-four-hour grocery store on Sawtelle Boulevard. It was brightly lit, and cars were coming and going.

Our school was easy to spot. It took up a whole square

block and was pitch-black. *Now, where to land?*

"The clock tower," Angela said as if she had heard the question in my head. The clock tower adorned the roof over the main entrance of the auditorium. It was flat on top.

As we glided forward, I concentrated on setting Sam down safely. He and Angela were positioned perfectly. Angela grabbed on and landed on her knees. In my concern about Sam, I forgot to squeeze myself in and was left hanging over the edge. I had to let go of Sam's hand, or I would have pulled him off. Without being tied to the others, I rose straight up like a ball full of air rushing to the surface of water. What a sensation of lightness and freedom! I made easy circles above my two companions.

"This is so cool!" I did a somersault. Angela and Sam stood up, laughing.

"I want to too," Sam called out, waving his arms in excitement.

"Come on," I said.

He was teetering on the edge of the tower and jumped without hesitation. He hovered for a second, then bobbed up. His robe billowed, and he looked like an umbrella from the waist down.

"Hey, watch me," I called over my shoulder. I dove and slapped the treetops that dotted the courtyard in the center of the school. Then I made a sharp turn and headed back, passing the clock tower on my left.

Sam was orbiting the tower. Angela was kneeling and watching.

"Come on, Angela," I said as I looped around. She didn't answer.

"What's wrong?" I said.

"I cannot jump."

"Angela, look at Sam. Did he fall? Here, I'll help you."

Angela stood. I glided toward her, but I couldn't stop midair. I grasped her hands, but instead of reversing myself to pull her toward me, I pushed her backward off the tower. Angela was on her back and floating like a sleeping person levitating out of bed. She gave a cry of indignation and began to thrash.

"You're fine." I laughed, letting go of her hands.

Angela flapped her arms and righted herself. "I suppose," she said.

I turned and pointed myself toward the sky. Below, Sam and Angela circled the auditorium. *They'll be okay for a few minutes. Sam is annoying, but Angela will stay with him.*

Higher and higher—the houses and cars got smaller and smaller. The cool air was delicious. *I can go anywhere.*

To the west, a bright star twinkled at me, and I headed for it. On my left, I could see jets landing at the Los Angeles International Airport. Like birds with green and red lights, they swooped down onto runways lined with glowing blue dots.

I zoomed on, the wind roaring in my ears. My body was a bullet—elbows locked, arms reaching, hands together like an arrow. My cheeks burned from the whipping cold air. Tears streamed my face. My fingers were numb with cold, but I didn't care.

I felt lonely and eager, determined and impatient. I was insane, but I didn't care about that either. In a flash of cosmic fusion, I longed to morph into the true Thea: strong, confident, happy.

The ocean was below me. It stretched out forever. On the horizon, the inky black sky melted into the sea. The steady wind on my face, the *whoosh* in my ears, the salt air in my lungs, all mixed together, and I was no longer sure if I was moving or holding still in a vast, starlit universe. My bright westerly star twinkled straight ahead. It was my friend, inviting me and keeping me company. *It's so beautiful. I could go on forever. So sleepy . . . Take a little nap . . .*

I closed my eyes. I knew I was falling, but my brain didn't register any danger. *I will crash into the black water. Will it be cold?*

Suddenly, a wave of nausea swept through me, and a voice inside my head screamed, *WAKE UP!* My eyes popped open. *I'm falling! I'm going to hit the water! I won't be able to fly! I'm going to drown!*

I thrust my arms left and my legs right and jerked my head up. Like a tight curve on a roller coaster, I was yanked up and left. My rushing descent halted, and the air, which a second before had refused to support me, now easily held me. I flew straight and steady. I was back in control.

That was a close call. The air must be too thin up there. I took deep, greedy breaths as I made my way toward the lights of the Santa Monica shoreline. I was glad when I reached the beach parking lot. I glided across the Pacific Coast Highway to the rows of fenced backyards that ran perpendicular to the beach and made my way back to Mar Vista.

How long was I gone? Angela and Sam will be worried. I hope they're still at the school. They wouldn't go back to the willow without me, would they? Up ahead —there's the school. There's the clock tower. Where are they?

I zipped over the school grounds, searching for my companions, then I returned to the clock tower. Grabbing on, I landed for the first time that night.

Where could they be? Did someone see them? I waited and worried. Finally, to the north, two oversized birds approached. As they got closer, I recognized the bulky brown bird with the billowy robe as my brother, and the slender blue bird at his side as my best friend.

They landed a lot less gracefully than two birds would have, clutching the edge of the tower and almost knocking me off.

"Thanks for abandoning us!" Angela said breathlessly. "We searched everywhere for you."

"I told you to follow me!"

"You did not," she replied.

"Maybe you didn't hear me."

"Maybe I did not want to blast off, straight up like a rocket."

"I wanted to see what I could do by myself. You won't believe what happened." I told them about my ocean adventure and then asked, "Where did you guys go?"

"Mostly, we waited for you," Angela said, turning her face away.

Angela is mad at me. So what? I'm not sorry.

"We should go back," Angela said. "It is late."

"This time, don't help," I ordered Sam. We held hands

and headed back, pulling Sam along between us.

We crossed Monroe Street and sailed over Mamac's front yard. When we passed over the driveway gate, a flash of light caught my eye. I pulled on Sam's hand and pointed.

On the ground below, a dark figure was standing in Mamac's driveway. *Who is that? What is he doing? Is he a burglar?* The figure pointed a flashlight at the duffel bag at his feet. He began pulling sheets of paper out of the bag and crumpling them into balls. Then he pulled off the wire screen that covered the opening to the crawl space under the house. He tossed the paper balls inside. A metal can gleamed in the light. There was a spark. Yellow flames shot up. Someone was burning Mamac's house!

Call for Help

"Take Sam to the tree," I whispered to Angela.

I zoomed away, kicking my feet as I went. *There's a gas station a few blocks from here. I think there's a phone booth there. It's so late. I don't think anyone will see me. Hurry! The house is burning right now!*

I was flying so fast, I could hardly breathe. *I've never made a call from a phone booth.* Memories of checking the coin return of every telephone booth I walked past for returned dimes flashed through my head. *I don't have a dime! Maybe it's free to call the fire department. Maybe the operator will help me. But what if I need a dime to call the operator?*

Suddenly, I was above the bright lights of Gateway and Barrington boulevards. Everything looked weird from above and strangely deserted. The glass phone booth stood on the corner exactly where I remembered it. A dim light inside shone on the black pay phone.

I overshot the corner and had to circle back. I pointed my arms and rushed head-first toward the ground, but as soon as I got close, I was swung into a perfect curve right back up into the air. *What's happening? I can't land! Dang! How does this work? If anyone comes along . . .*

I bent at the waist and thrust my feet toward Earth. That jerked me upright—but I was standing ten feet above the ground!

Down Gateway, the headlights of a car lumbered in my direction. Like a huge, insane bird, I flapped my arms and kicked, struggling against the air. It felt like trying to stand on the bottom of the deep-end of a swimming pool. When my toes finally brushed the ground, gravity hit me like a bowling ball. I collapsed.

The headlights were a block away now. I stood up. My feet tingled and hurt at the same time. I hobbled to a gas pump and hid behind it. The car passed the gas station.

I limped to the phone booth, went inside, and pulled the glass door shut. I picked up the receiver. *Please work.* I held my breath and dialed *O. It's ringing!*

"Operator. We're here to help," a woman's voice said.

"There's a fire—can you call the fire department?"

"Please hold."

Please hold? Oh my gosh!

"Los Angeles Fire Department is on the line."

"What is the address of your emergency?" It was a man's voice. He sounded very serious.

"There's a fire. A house is on fire."

"Address?"

"5154 Monroe Street."

"A fire truck has been dispatched to that location. Are

you inside the house?"

"Me? Um—no, I'm not in the house."

"Who is in the house?"

"No one. It's empty. I mean, it's not empty, but there's no one there."

"Your name?"

"I have to go."

"Stay on the phone," he directed. "You're in a phone booth, right?"

He knows I'm in a phone booth? How does he know that? "I have to go," I repeated.

I hung up on the dispatcher and stared at the telephone. *I shouldn't hang up on a grown-up, but I couldn't tell him who I am. What difference does it make anyway? I have to get back to Angela and Sam.*

Back on the sidewalk, I jumped and flapped, and jumped and flapped, and ran and jumped and flapped, but each time, I landed right back on the cement. I even climbed on top of a parked car and leapt as high as I could. *Bam!* I hit the ground.

I'll have to run back to Mamac's. If another car comes, I'll hide. I took off running as fast as I could. I didn't stop until I reached Monroe Street. Mamac's house was two blocks down. *Why don't I hear sirens? Maybe that man on the phone didn't believe me because I hung up on him. Hey! I might run smack into the bad guy who started the fire! He could be anywhere.*

I swerved onto a neighbor's lawn and crouched below a window. My heart was racing. *Think, Thea.* I pushed my hair out of my face. My hands were shaking.

I must get back to the willow before the fire trucks

come. *I have to hurry, but I can't run into Him—the bad guy.* That thought made my heart start racing again. *Calm. I'm calm. I'll go fast, but I won't go down Mamac's driveway. He could still be there. I'll get into the backyard from this side—over the fence. He won't be there—unless he goes there to hide—but why would he do that? No, he's either in the driveway, or he's running away. I can't waste any more time!*

I crept to the edge of the sidewalk and peered down the block. Empty. The air smelled smoky. I hunched over and hugged the shadows as I hurried toward Mamac's.

A tall cedar fence stood between Mamac's and her neighbor's house. Another fence ran perpendicular to it, enclosing a narrow side yard on each side. On Mamac's side, the fence was mostly hidden by the avocado tree. I hurried up the walkway. It was a relief to step behind the tree and not feel so exposed. I stood on tiptoe and tried to grab the top of the fence slats. *I can't reach it. It's too high.* I stepped back, and my leg bumped something hard. It was the electric meter attached to Mamac's house.

I climbed onto it and tried again, grabbing the top of the fence with my hands and using my tennis-shoed feet against the slats for traction. Once my weight was over the top, there was no stopping me—I fell to the ground behind the fence. That's when I heard the sirens.

It was very dark. I had never been back there before. I could see the neighbor's windows above the fence—closer than I had imagined. As I crept toward Mamac's backyard, ancient leaves crunched under my feet. *Quieter, Thea! The neighbors are sleeping right inside those windows. And the bad guy—don't think about him!*

At the back corner of the house, a large pyracantha bush blocked my way into the yard. Its leaves had corners with points like needles, and its stiff stems were spiked with thorns. Even through my sweatshirt, the branches clawed me as I forced my way past. My fingers brushed soft, sticky cobwebs, and I imagined spiders dropping into my hair.

I pushed through the last barbed branch, tripped on a brick, and stumbled into Mamac's back garden. I jammed my fingers into my out-of-control hair and shook it, trying to dislodge any twigs (or spiders) that might have fallen in.

The air was heavy now with sweet, suffocating smoke. It tasted foul on my tongue and made my nose stuffy. *Dang! I hope the smoke doesn't give Sam an asthma attack. I'm sure he doesn't have his inhaler with him.*

I peered into the recess of the yard. A row of tall, spindly bushes lined the fence all the way to the back corner. *They look like soldiers standing guard.* Just then a gust of wind blew, making the bushes swing their branches like overgrown arms completely out of sync with each other. *They hear the sirens and are freaking out, signaling with wild waving.* An image of *Felix the Cat* popped into my head. Felix, walking along, not paying attention, whistling. *The soldier bushes are warning me: Danger! Scram! Stay out! Crazy magic and scary bad guy here!*

I never knew the name of those bushes, but we kids were sure that their purple, cherry-sized fruit was poisonous. I crouched and crept forward. *Please protect me, poison soldiers.*

The sirens were screaming when I reached the back

corner of the garden. The willow tree was directly across, on the other side of the yard. I hesitated. *I hope Angela and Sam made it to the tree. If the bad guy caught them* . . . A shiver ran through me. I glanced toward Mamac's house. Flashing red lights lit the sky. The sirens stopped.

I'll make a run for the willow. I lifted my foot to step away from the protection of the soldier bushes. *CRACK!* It was the sound of a stick breaking under someone's weight.

I froze. *It's him! He's here. Maybe he saw me. He might be coming to grab me right now!* I wanted to scream and run away. I looked around, but couldn't see anyone. *Keep going, Thea.* I stepped onto the dichondra and moved along the back fence line until I was right behind the willow tree.

I dashed forward. There was a rustling sound, then a *"huff,"* like someone out of breath. Through the curtain of leaves, the trunk stood thick and strong, waiting for me. I leapt into the cradle where the massive branches forked. I had never climbed the willow from the back, and my feet slipped and scuffed the trunk as I pulled myself up. I jammed my foot into a crevice and climbed.

Above me, moonlight filtered through the limbs and lit the top of Angela's blonde hair. Sam's bulky silhouette was crouched below her. Angela started waving her arms to warn me of the intruder below. *She looks like one of the poison soldiers.* She put her finger to her lips.

I wasn't up very high, and anyone who entered the circle of willow leaves could easily have seen me. I peered through the branches, trying to see who was in the garden.

SNAP. CRUNCH. There—by the back fence.

"*Uhhhf!*" A bulky bag emerged into a patch of moonlight and toppled over the fence, disappearing into Mrs. Oxford's yard with a thud. Then a hand shot out of the dark and grabbed the fence top. In one liquid movement, a figure appeared, twisted, and dropped over the fence. In that split second, before he dropped out of sight, I got a glimpse of his face.

I climbed up to Angela and Sam.

"Did you see him?" I whispered.

"Yes. That must be the person we saw in the driveway," Angela said.

"But did you see his face?" I asked.

"Uncle Ray," Sam said.

"Did you see his face, Angela?"

"Yes, but I never met your uncle. I do not know what he looks like."

Suddenly, bouncing beams of light appeared at the back of the house. Three figures carrying flashlights ran back and forth. Their bright beams shot across the house, then they hurried back up the driveway.

"We better climb higher," I whispered.

We settled where we could sit together—two branches below the invisible staircase. We waited. I felt a small hand on my shoulder and hot breath in my ear.

"I have to pee." It was Sam.

"No!" Angela whispered fiercely.

"Thea, I have to pee," he repeated.

"You can't pee now. You have to hold it," I said.

"If they catch us here, they are going to say we started the fire," Angela said.

That hadn't occurred to me. She's right! Of course

they will think that. Why else would we be here in the middle of the night while the house is on fire?

"We're not going to get caught," I said. "Not if we stay put and keep quiet. Sam, just hold it till they're gone."

"I can't. I've been holding it a long time already."

"Well, hurry up then. You can pee off this branch. We won't look," I whispered.

"No, no, no," Angela murmured.

Sam didn't move.

"Hurry, Sam. They might come back and search the yard," I said.

"Okay," he said doubtfully. I looked away but held his arm, in case he lost his balance. The urine had a musty smell and made a faint, splattering sound.

Sam had barely finished when the figures with the flashlights appeared at the back of the house again and headed down the garden path. When they reached the clothesline, two fanned out, searching the perimeter of the yard with their bright beams. The third figure came straight toward the willow tree.

"Please, no . . . " Angela whispered.

We barely dared to breathe. The figure pushed aside the leaves and stood below us. His light swept the ground around him, then it scanned the lower branches of the tree, right where I had been perched moments before.

"All clear over here," a voice from across the yard called out.

"It's clear here too," the man below replied. He rejoined his companions, and the three men ran back up to the house and disappeared around the side.

We waited. We couldn't see the fire from where we

were, but we heard the firefighters shouting, and the lights from their trucks made the sky flash red for a whole block. It felt like forever before the flashing stopped, and all became quiet again. My legs were half asleep, and my bottom hurt from sitting on the branch.

"I am cold," Angela said.

"Me too," Sam said, yawning.

"I think they left," I said.

"Huh?" Sam said sleepily.

"We must get home," Angela said.

We climbed down, ran across the dichondra to the brick path, and up to the house. In the driveway, it stunk like the smoky wet wood of a smoldering campfire. Sam sneezed.

Even in the predawn light, we could see the pink stucco splashed with black stains all the way to the roof. I knelt on the driveway and examined the charred opening of the crawl space where the fire had been started.

"What's this?" Something wet and clingy was hanging from the broken wood. I pulled it off. "It's a piece of cloth," I muttered.

"We must go now," Angela said.

I stuffed the cloth into the pocket of my jeans. Sam started rubbing his eyes, trying to fight back tears. I felt like crying too.

"It'll be okay, Sam," I said, miserably.

"My goodness," Angela said. She put her arms around our shoulders. "There is nothing more to do tonight. We must return to your apartment before the sun rises."

"You're right." I sniffed. "Let's go. Wait. Let's make sure there's no one out front. I'll bet the whole neighborhood was watching."

We opened the gate a few inches—just enough for three sets of eyes to peer out. The street was empty.

"Guess they went to bed," Sam said.

We slipped out of the gate and ran home—stopping only to catch our breath before crossing National Boulevard. Sam had left the front door of our apartment unlocked. We slipped inside. He plopped onto the couch in the living room. Angela and I tiptoed to my bedroom.

Mom's door was open and she lay fast asleep in her bed. It was almost six o'clock, and I was exhausted. I put on my nightie and wiggled into my sleeping bag.

"Good night, Thea," Angela whispered. She giggled. "Maybe I should say, *good morning,* instead."

"Hey, Angela. Something really weird happened after I called the fire department."

"What happened?"

"I tried to fly back to the tree, but it didn't work."

"What did not work?"

"I couldn't fly. I tried for a long time. I had to run back to Mamac's house on foot."

"Hmm, I wonder why."

"I think we can only fly from the invisible staircase or a high place where we landed."

"Rightly so." she murmured.

"You can't just take off from the ground—nothing special about the ground."

"Indeed not."

"Not part of the magic."

Angela didn't say anything. She had fallen asleep.

The Break-in

We slept until eleven. When we came out to the kitchen looking for breakfast, the expression on Mom's face told me she had gotten the news.

"Good morning," she said, without smiling.

The French toast she served us was delicious. Sam and I smothered ours in butter and syrup. Angela had one piece—dry.

As soon as we had eaten, Mom said, "It's time for Angela to go home. It was so nice to have you with us, hon."

"Thank you for having me, Mrs. MacRobert." Angela gave Mom a hug. I never saw her hug her own mother (and I sure as heck never hugged Mrs. V), but Angela liked to give Mom a hug now and then. It usually put Mom in a good mood—but not this morning.

I carried Angela's sleeping bag to the front door and whispered in her ear, "I'll send you a note when I can."

The moment Angela was out the door, Mom started pacing. "Something has happened," she said. "I received a phone call from the police this morning. One of Mamac's neighbors gave them our number. There was a fire—someone intentionally set fire to Mamac's house last night. Fortunately, someone called the fire department, and they were able to put it out before it destroyed the place." Mom paused and rubbed her forehead with the back of her hand. "They asked me about you kids being over there or if you play with matches. I told them you were here, and besides, you would never do such a thing." Mom walked into the kitchen and stood, lost in thought, staring out the window.

I felt my face get hot.

"We would never do such a thing?" Sam said. He was sitting on the couch, and I kicked his foot. "What, Thea? We didn't make the fire. We just—"

"Mom knows we didn't make the fire, Sam. Just let her talk." I kicked him again and glared at him.

"Mom?" I said. She was still staring out the kitchen window. "Mom!"

She turned around. "What, honey?"

"Uncle Ray wouldn't want to burn Mamac's house, would he?"

Mom opened her mouth as if she were going to speak then closed it and stared at me. "Why do you ask that?"

"You were talking to him on the phone after Mamac's funeral. I thought he was mad that we were going to move into her house."

Mom came over to where I was standing. She took my hands in hers. She looked really scared.

"Thea," she said. "Oh God. Yes! No . . . ." Her voice

trailed off as her thoughts raced ahead. "Would he—could he do such a thing?" She dropped my hands and started pacing again.

"I told you Mamac's will states that we can live in her house until Sam graduates high school. That's not for another ten years. That's when her house will pass legally and permanently to Ray. In the meantime, Mamac left Ray her entire life insurance policy—ten thousand dollars. Not a fortune, but it makes up for not inheriting her house right away. If the house were to burn, I suppose Ray might try to get his hands on the fire insurance money. He could take us to court, or threaten to, and turn everything into a legal mess." Mom stopped pacing and stomped her foot. "He is too despicable!"

"Maybe you should tell this to the police," I said.

"I don't have any proof. No proof. Just like before when—" Mom glanced at Sam.

She wants to say, just like before when your dad died. But she won't say it in front of Sam. I flopped onto the couch next to my little brother. *Maybe I shouldn't have told Mom that I heard Uncle Ray whispering, "I'm sorry, Howie," and, "It's all my fault," at Dad's funeral. I thought I was helping. I thought some grown-up would put everything back to normal. But that didn't happen. No one could have made it right. Even if we knew what Uncle Ray knows, it still wouldn't be okay. Dad would still be—*

"Can we go look at it?" Sam asked.

"I went at nine o'clock—right after I got the call," Mom replied. "I suppose you two may go if you go together. Under no circumstances are you to go inside the house. The damage is along the driveway side. Don't touch anything, and come right back."

Sam and I went to our room. I scribbled a note for Angela and sped it over on the pulley, jerking the line when it reached her window to tap the glass.

Angela, We have to talk!!!

❀ Thea ❀

A minute later the reply came.

Dear Thea,

 I can meet you on top of the carport in ten minutes.

❀ Love, Angela ❀

"I'm going too," Sam said.

"Of course," I said as if it were normal for Sam to meet Angela with me. *He's in this mess with us. There's no changing that.*

"Cool!" Sam said.

Out in the alley, Sam followed me up the dumpster ladder. I balanced on the rim and gave him a boost onto the carport roof. Angela was waiting for us. She stared at Sam but didn't say anything. We sat cross-legged in a circle, and I filled her in on what Mom had told us.

"I want to climb the tree and fly!" Sam blurted.

"Jumping Jehoshaphat!" Angela exclaimed.

"Jumping what?" Sam asked.

"Samuel, it is daytime! Do you want everyone to see us?" Angela said.

"Besides, Sam," I said, "we need to think about the house. Don't you care that someone is trying to burn it down? Hey, that reminds me, why did you say to Mom, 'We didn't set the fire. We just—' We just what?"

Sam stared at me like he was caught with his hand in the cookie jar. "Just . . . We just—nothing. I wasn't going to say nothing. I don't know—I don't remember."

We climbed down to the alley and started walking to Mamac's. I was wearing the same pants I had worn the night before. I reached into my pocket and said, "Hey you guys, I still have this rag that was hanging in the opening under Mamac's house." I held it up. Half of it was burned and dirty with soot. The other half was a faded red, and its edge was finished with stitching.

"What is it?" Sam asked.

"Obviously, it is a clue," Angela said. "The arsonist must have used it."

"The what?" Sam asked.

"The arsonist. The person who set the fire," Angela said.

"I was thinking that too. The bad guy left it there. I've seen this kind of cloth before. My dad kept a bunch of them in the garage of our old house—for working on the car. You know, to clean greasy stuff."

"We should check if there are more of them at Mamac's," Angela said.

Mamac's house looked worse in the midday light. The stucco along the driveway side was black from top to bottom, and all three windows were broken. I leaned over and laced my fingers together to make a step for Sam.

"Hop up," I ordered.

Sam stepped onto my cupped hands, and I lifted him so he could peer into the window at the back corner of the house.

"P.U. It stinks!" he said.

I looked up at Angela and rolled my eyes. "What do you *see*, Sam?"

"Mamac's sewing room and broken glass."

Sam hopped down.

"Mom doesn't want to tell the police that she thinks Uncle Ray did this because she doesn't have any proof."

As I said this, an idea crept into my brain. I tried to ignore it, but it wouldn't go away. Sharp tingles pecked the back of my neck. *I better not say it out loud, or we could really get in trouble.* But my idea had a life of its own and had already jumped into Sam's brain.

"Let's go to Uncle Ray's and look for more red towels!" he said.

"Good grief, Samuel. Are we going to knock on his door and say, excuse us, dear sir, but we would like to search your house for red cloth so that the authorities may send you to prison?" Angela said.

"Well, we don't gotta say, 'dear sir,'" Sam declared.

The tingling in my neck moved down my spine and a jumpy kind of fear gurgled in my stomach. Now that the idea had been said out loud, it was hard to resist.

"We could—" I said.

"Thea! You said your uncle is bad," Angela said.

"We could walk over there, and if his car's not there, we could look around. We won't do anything stupid," I replied.

"Do you know what his car looks like?" Angela asked.

"I know where his parking space is. It's in front of his back door. Don't worry. If he's home, we won't go near the place."

We walked to Sawtelle Boulevard. The blocks became super long, but we finally got to Pico Blvd. On the corner of Sawtelle and Pico, a sign said, *Cozy Court*. But there was nothing cozy about it. It was a dirty-beige, stuccoed bungalow with six apartments. A pack of kids, one in a sagging diaper, played on a patch of crabgrass in front. Cars on Pico and Sawtelle whizzed by, and the cold gray concrete of the San Diego Freeway loomed overhead.

A long driveway ran behind the bungalow. Along it were parking spaces—one per apartment—in front of each back door.

"This is it," I said.

"Which one is his?" Angela asked.

"The one with the red door. He's not home. If he were, his car would be right there in that spot," I said.

I led us, single file, down the alley. Each apartment was the same, except their back doors were painted different colors. I knew Uncle Ray's door was red because I had visited once with Dad. Blue, yellow, green—we ducked as we passed each neighbor's window. At the red door, I climbed the three wooden steps and peered through the frosted louvered window. The interior looked blurry because of the glass. Blurry, but unlit and still. I tried the doorknob. It was locked.

"Hey, that window is open," Sam said, pointing to the sliding window to the right of the door.

I reached over and pulled the bottom of the window

screen with my fingertips. It was hinged at the top and swung out easily.

"I can fit," Sam said.

"Should we?" Angela asked.

"Since Uncle Ray is family, it's not breaking in. We're not going to steal anything," I said.

"True," Angela said, hesitating. "But Thea, what if he returns?"

"He's not here now, so he can't catch us, right?"

"Right . . ." Angela said, glancing down the alley.

"We have to do it. He might go back and burn the rest of Mamac's house! The police need proof, or they can't do anything. We need to find proof in Uncle Ray's apartment."

"Jumping Josy-fat! We going or not?" Sam said.

"Please, Angela," I said.

"Very well. We shall do it! The Nancy Drew Duo—I mean, The Nancy Drew Trio," she corrected, "is on the scene. I will be the sentry and guard the door. If your uncle returns, I will alert you, and we will flee out the front door."

"I'm not scared," Sam declared. "Give me a boost. I'll climb through the window and let you in."

I cupped my hands for Sam's foot. He stepped up and slid through the window headfirst. *Thump. Click.* The door opened.

"I will be right here, watching," Angela said, posting herself inside the back door.

Sam and I stood in the kitchen. It smelled of greasy food that had been sitting too long. Dirty TV dinner trays and Chinese takeout boxes were scattered across the countertop. The garbage pail overflowed with empty beer bottles.

In the living room sat the ugliest couch I had ever seen. It might have been orange at one time, but now its arms had a dirty-brown sheen, and the cushions were sagging and stained. In front of it was a coffee table with a brown telephone and an ashtray filled with cigarette butts.

"Let's check the bedroom," I said.

A short hall led to two doors. The first was open. A mattress lay on the floor—a green blanket twisted up on one side. The closet door was open, but the closet was empty. It was a lonely room, and I couldn't help feeling sorry for Uncle Ray. *I wish my family wasn't so messed up.*

"Let's keep going," Sam said, pulling me back into the hall.

"This must be the bathroom," I said.

Sam opened the door, and we crowded inside.

"Stinks!" Sam said.

I scanned the room: grungy sink, faucet dripping, gross toilet needing flushing, plastic shower curtain peppered with black mold. I jerked the curtain aside. On the floor of the shower was a big red gas can. Red rags and newspapers were stacked on top of it. The fumes were noxious, and I felt dizzy.

"I can't breathe too good," Sam said in a choked voice.

We backed out of the bathroom and started back down the hall. Suddenly, Angela appeared, her face wild with panic.

"He is here!" she squealed.

A car door slammed.

"Let's go!" I said. We ran to the living room and raced to the front door. I grabbed the doorknob. It turned, but the door didn't budge. "There's a separate lock. You need a key to get out!"

The back door banged shut. Boots on linoleum.

"He is coming!" Angela whispered frantically.

The couch was to my left. I dropped to my knees and scrambled behind it. Sam and Angela followed.

We listened and waited. The refrigerator door opened, then shut. *Click. Pshh.* I imagined a beer bottle being opened.

More footsteps. Then, footsteps muted by carpet. He was in the living room. The striking of a match. The smell of sulfur. The couch creaked as someone sat. I crooked my neck to look. The back of a head—shaggy black hair. It was Uncle Ray, and he was inches from our hiding place!

Cigarette smoke rose gray and cloudy as he puffed and exhaled. He let out a big sigh. Heels thumped the floor. He had stretched out his legs.

The telephone rang.

"Yeah?" Uncle Ray said, springing to his feet. "Bruno, I was about to call you. I've got ten grand already. I swear. Where do you want to meet? . . . Okay." Footsteps. Uncle Ray was pacing in front of the couch. "The other ten—I'm working on. I thought I had it handled, but I was interrupted. I need a little more time. . . . Just a week." He hung up. "Geez," he muttered.

More pacing. Another match. Another cigarette.

I heard a faint rattling sound in my left ear. I had just enough room to turn my head and see Sam staring at the back of the couch in front of his face. *He's wheezing! It's the dang cigarette smoke! Did he bring his inhaler? He couldn't pull it out of his pocket anyway, all scrunched up behind this couch.*

Within seconds, Sam's lungs weren't just wheezing on the exhale, they made a clogged, whistling sound on the inhale too. *We have to get out of here!* I stared at Sam. His mouth hung open, and the raspy rattle from his lungs grew louder. He raised his hand and covered his mouth to stifle a cough. Dread ran through me like an electric current.

The pacing stopped. Uncle Ray was standing still in the middle of the room.

"What the . . . ?"

The couch squeaked, and Uncle Ray's face appeared over its back. He looked surprised, then mad—very mad.

"What in blazes are you doing back there?" he shouted.

Angela screamed and scrambled out from her end of the couch. I bolted from my end. Sam tried to follow me, but Uncle Ray had caught the shoulder of his T-shirt. Sam struggled to get away and started coughing. The couch made it hard for Uncle Ray to get hold of him with both hands.

"Hold still!" Uncle Ray shouted. "You're not going anywhere."

Angela stood in the kitchen doorway, watching in terror. I wanted to escape with her, but I couldn't leave Sam. Uncle Ray had hold of him with both hands now and was dragging him over the back of the couch.

I have to do something!

I rushed at Uncle Ray and kicked him in the side of the knee as hard as I could. He took one hand off Sam and grabbed my upper arm. That gave Sam a chance to wiggle loose.

"Run!" I shouted. But Sam didn't move. He just stood there with his mouth hanging open, wheezing.

"Samuel!" Angela cried from the kitchen doorway. She ran into the living room and grabbed him by the wrist. Sam never took his eyes off me as Angela pulled him from the living room. They disappeared through the kitchen door.

Uncle Ray was squeezing my upper arm so hard it felt like he was crushing the bone. He pushed me onto the couch and held me there, his face red with fury. He raised his free hand.

He's going to slap me!

I grabbed the burning cigarette from the ashtray on the coffee table and ground it into the soft underside of Uncle Ray's arm. Red-hot tobacco scattered onto my legs and burned me through my jeans.

It took a few seconds for Uncle Ray's brain to register what was happening. By the time he looked at his arm, I could smell searing flesh. He howled with pain and jerked his arm back. I leapt to my feet and dashed to the kitchen. I flew through the open back door, jumped the porch steps, and landed in the alley. Angela and Sam were there, not wanting to abandon me, but not daring to reenter the bungalow.

"Run!" I screamed.

Escape

We raced down the alley, pulling Sam between us.

"Brats!" Uncle Ray shouted. I didn't look back. At the end of the alley, we turned onto Pico and kept running. When we reached Sawtelle, the streetlight was green, so we crossed and ran down Sawtelle. Halfway down the block were the railroad tracks. We ran across those too. By then we were completely out of breath, so we stopped. The sidewalk stretched out empty behind us.

"Let's go in that lot," I said, panting and pointing to the parking lot behind the liquor store on the corner. We dashed into the lot and ducked behind a parked car. Sam sat on the concrete block at the head of a parking space. He put his face between his knees, coughed, and started wheezing again—even worse than before. Angela and I sat on either side of him, and I patted him on the back.

"Hey, Sam. It's okay. Have you got your inhaler?"

Sam reached into his pocket and pulled out the white

device. He took a big breath as he squeezed it twice, sucking the medicine into his lungs. Within a minute, he was sitting up straight and breathing normally.

"We can call Mom to come get you," I said.

"No way! It was just 'cause of that stinky stuff in the shower and that gross cigarette. Uncle Ray is a maniac. He almost got us!"

"Why didn't you give us more warning?" I asked Angela.

"I told you, I never met your uncle. A brown car came down the alley, but I did not know it belonged to him until he parked in front of the red door."

"And the front door—whoever made a lock like that? You need a key to get out of the house!" I said.

"Did you find anything?" Angela asked.

"Gas can, newspapers, red rags in the shower," I said.

"So, he is the arsonist," Angela replied.

"We should tell Mommy," Sam said.

"I don't want to tell Mom. She would be mad at me for letting you climb through Uncle Ray's window," I said.

"I want Mommy. I mean, I want to tell her," Sam said.

"We shouldn't have let you come. You want to tell Mom we were at Mamac's last night too." Sam started to cry. "Sam, stop it. You'll start wheezing again."

"I'm not gonna tell. Wild horses couldn't drag it out of me. I won't tell Mommy unless she asks me."

Angela jumped to her feet. "You cannot tell your mommy!" she shouted. "If you do, she will tell my parents!"

I stood up and grabbed Angela's arm and pulled her a few feet away. "We can't trust him," I whispered. "He's going to say something to my mom, and she'll ask him questions, and he'll blab the whole thing."

"We should have sent him home last night," Angela said.

"I have an idea. Go along with what I say."

"But—" Angela didn't get to finish her sentence because I returned to my seat on the concrete block next to Sam.

"Now listen, Sam. You have to listen real good, okay?" I said.

"I already told you, wild horses—"

"Listen up! All that stuff last night? Forget it. There is no such thing as an invisible staircase, and kids can't fly."

I gave Angela a *help me* look over Sam's head.

"Yes—just—just a story," Angela stammered. "Thea and I told you a fairytale about three children, and we said they were us."

"Right," I said. "The children climbed a tree in the night, and found an invisible staircase, and were blasted into the air, and flew around. It was really fun, but it was just a story."

"Of course it was," Angela agreed. "We never did that."

"Or, maybe you had a dream—a really cool dream about flying," I said.

Sam's head went back and forth as he listened—brown eyes stared intently at me, then Angela, then me again.

"Or, a game. It was a game we played. All make-believe," Angela said, clapping her hands and smiling.

"And," I added, "when you feel like telling Mom, remember this: she won't believe you. She'll think you're making it up, and she'll be mad at you. You don't want

Mom to be mad at you, do you? We went to Uncle Ray's house because Mom thought he might have started the fire. Mom needs our help."

"Right," Sam said. "We want to help Mommy."

I looked at Angela. My unspoken question was, *will this work?* She nodded and shrugged.

"Uncle Ray said his plan was interrupted. He wants to go back and set another fire. He might even go back tonight. Mom can't stop him. Who do you think can stop him?"

"The president?" Sam said.

"No!" I said.

"Who then?" Sam said.

The police can stop him," I said.

"Oh my goodness," Angela said. "Do we have to?"

"Who else can help us?" I said.

"I do not even know where the police station is," Angela said.

"We drive by it with Mom sometimes. There's a bunch of police cars parked outside. It's that way," I said, pointing.

We headed west. We used side streets and kept careful watch in case Uncle Ray was looking for us in his car. After eight blocks, we stopped in a market and asked the clerk.

"Two blocks. Left on Butler," the clerk said, pointing and eyeing us suspiciously.

The police station was a two-story box. We stood in front of the entrance, staring at it. The thick glass doors were tinted green, and we couldn't see inside.

"You had better do the talking. He is your relation," Angela said.

"Okay." I inhaled a breath of determination.

We entered. Cool air engulfed us, and I realized how sweltering it was outside. Fluorescent lighting cast a blue-white hue on the reception area. It was quiet, and at first, I thought no one was around. Then I saw the policeman in a navy-blue uniform sitting at a desk behind the counter.

The countertop was as tall as Sam who started jumping up and down to get a peek at the seated officer. "We come about the fire," he blurted as he sprung into the air. "It was Uncle Ray."

"Yes," Angela affirmed. "We, I mean they, found proof in his house—I mean apartment. Actually, I think Mother would call it a California bungalow, although I am not sure about that. You would need to ask her—I mean, please do not ask her. I will just say, domicile. The gas can, and the red rags, and the—what was it?" She looked at me for help.

"Newspapers. Red rags and newspapers. We want you to go arrest him before he gets rid of the evidence," I said.

"Yeah, *ebidence*," Jumping-Sam chimed in. "*Ebidence* of the *arborist!*"

"Heavens to Betsy! Samuel, will you be quiet?" Angela scolded. "An arborist is someone who takes care of trees. You mean arsonist."

"Hey, you said not to talk about the tree! Thea, did you hear her? Mr. Policeman, that was a story they told me. There was no tree and no in-divisible staircase."

The desk sergeant stared.

"It's our uncle," I said. "We found—"

"I climbed through the window," Sam said loudly.

"But we were not breaking in. The uncle is family," Angela offered.

Again, I tried to explain, but Sam kept jumping and interrupting, Angela kept trying to help, and we all ended up talking at once.

A policeman with olive skin and jet-black hair entered from one of the doorways behind the desk. "What's up?" he said to the seated officer.

"They say they know about a fire. Want me to call their parents?"

"Call our parents?" I said. "What good will that do? Angela will get in trouble. And Mom—we're trying to help her. Don't call her!"

The standing policeman stared at me and frowned. "Don't call them yet," he said. "I'll check with Mark." He left, and in a moment, a man in a gray suit entered.

"This is Detective Brightwell. He is an arson investigator. You can tell him about your fire," the desk sergeant said.

"It's not *our* fire," Sam said indignantly. "It belongs to Uncle Ray!"

Detective Brightwell looked us up and down. "Come with me," he said. He flipped up a section of the counter so we could pass. Then he led us around the desk, through a door, down a hall, and into a room. There was a long table with chairs around it. "Have a seat," he said.

I sat. Angela and Sam sat across from me, and Detective Brightwell sat at the head of the table. He was about Mom's age—old, but still young. He had dark blond hair, and his blue-gray eyes had laugh lines at the outside corners.

"You," he said, looking at me. "Start at the beginning."

I told him about the scrap of red rag we had found at

Mamac's, and what we saw in Uncle Ray's shower, and the phone call.

"How much is ten grand?" Sam interrupted. "Is it ten dollars?"

"No. It is ten thousand dollars, and it is impolite to interrupt," Angela said.

"Uncle Ray told—I think his name was Bruno—that he would give him ten grand."

"Bruno? First or last name?"

"He just said Bruno. Mom told me that my uncle is getting ten thousand dollars from my grandmother's life insurance. She thinks he might be trying to get more money by burning my grandmother's house," I said.

"And why does your uncle need so much money?" Detective Brightwell asked.

"Uncle Ray is bad. My dad got shot and he—" I looked at Sam and stopped speaking.

"Shot?" the detective said, his eyes widening.

"Yes. We don't know who—" *Why am I whispering? He thinks we're just kids, and we don't know anything. How can I make him understand?*

I sat up straight and cleared my throat. "I don't know why Uncle Ray needs so much money. I just know that he's the one who set the fire."

"You're talking about the fire last night at 5154 Monroe Street?" he asked.

"Yes," I said.

"Stay put." Detective Brightwell stood up and left the room. The three of us sat in worried silence. When he came back, he was holding a file.

"You did the right thing coming here," he said. "This is

my case. We found pieces of red rag at the fire site too. But it was dangerous and wrong of you to break into someone's house, even if he is your uncle. The police cannot break into this man's house. We would need a search warrant signed by a judge."

"How long does that take?" I asked.

"Maybe two hours. Maybe two days. Depends." The detective pushed a piece of paper and a pen across the table to me. "I want each of you to write your name, address, and telephone number on this paper. I'll have Officer Lomax give you a lift home."

"You have to do something now! Since he knows we were in his house, he's going to hide the rags and the gas. By the time you get your search warrant thingy, everything will be gone," I said.

"Yeah, and after he hides his stuff, he's gonna come after us," Sam said, tears glistening in his eyes.

"You're smart kids," Detective Brightwell said. "If he's our bad guy, he will likely remove the evidence from his house. I'll tell you what—let's take a ride over there. You kids will stay in the car and identify him for us. Officer Lomax and I will talk to him. He might even let us in his house. Criminals can be kind of stupid that way. No offense. I know he's related to you, but sometimes suspects give us permission to come in without a search warrant. Or, if he admits to being at the Monroe house last night, we can bring him in for questioning, and he won't have a chance to remove anything before we obtain a search warrant."

The detective stood up, but something in the file caught his eye. He leaned forward, planting his palms on the table.

"This report says the fire department dispatch was contacted at two forty-six a.m. by the *O* operator who had an anonymous tipper on the line. The tipper was calling from a phone booth. The dispatcher noted that the caller was likely a child and probably female."

"How do they know the call came from a phone booth?" Angela asked.

"When a person calls the operator, the phone number automatically displays. All phone booths in Los Angeles have a nine as their third number. This phone booth is at the corner of Barrington and Gateway." He gave me and Angela a swift, piercing look and waited. My face burned.

"So?" I said. *He'd never believe me if I tried to explain, and besides, I swore never to tell.*

"So, what do you know about that?" Detective Brightwell prodded.

"It's a good thing this person called the fire department, right?" I asked.

"Of course," he replied.

"Then whoever it was, we should be grateful to her—or him."

"Fair enough," he said. "You're a tough little girl, but my gut tells me you kids are trying to do the right thing. We'll drop that part of the mystery—at least for now."

*T*o protect and to serve was painted in black letters on the white door of the police car. We kids piled in the back seat. Officer Lomax sat in the driver's seat, and Detective Brightwell sat next to him.

"Ugh, this is where the criminals sit," Angela said.

"Cool," Sam said. He touched the stiff wire mesh separating the front seat from the rear. "This is so the bad guys don't hit the cops on the head."

The car was stifling. I reached out to roll down my window, but there was no window crank on the door—no door handle either. I tapped on the wire mesh, "Could you please roll down the windows?"

"Sure thing," Officer Lomax said. The back windows rolled down half way. "What's your uncle's address?"

"I don't know," I said. "It's called Cozy Court. It's on Pico, by the freeway."

"Cozy Court? I know it," Officer Lomax replied.

We rode in silence. My upper arm was throbbing. I hadn't told Detective Brightwell about Uncle Ray squeezing my arm.

We drove down Pico, and Cozy Court appeared on our left. Officer Lomax drove right by it, but I got a glimpse down the long driveway behind the bungalow. Uncle Ray was standing by his car. He threw a bundle into the trunk and ran up his apartment steps.

"There he is!" I shouted.

Officer Lomax made a quick U-turn and pulled into the driveway. He stopped behind Uncle Ray's car, blocking it from leaving. He shut off the motor and got out.

"Stay put," Detective Brightwell ordered as he exited the car. The two officers peered into the open trunk of Uncle Ray's Monte Carlo. I felt sick to my stomach.

Uncle Ray appeared at his back door carrying a pile of newspapers. He froze. His eyes darted from the two policemen, to the open trunk of his car, and then to the black-and-white patrol car with the three of us sitting in the back seat.

"Good afternoon, Ray. I am Detective Brightwell, and this is Officer Lomax."

"What do you want?"

"You have a gas can in your trunk and flammable materials in your arms. What do you know about the fire last night on Monroe Street?" Detective Brightwell said.

"The cops already called this morning. All I know is what they told me."

"What's the gas for, Ray?" Officer Lomax asked.

"It's for my car. I told you, I only know what the cops told me."

As Uncle Ray spoke, Detective Brightwell took a step toward him. Uncle Ray took a step back onto the threshold of his doorway. Suddenly, there was a blur of arms and white chaos as Uncle Ray threw the newspapers into the air between himself and the officers.

Angela screamed. Uncle Ray disappeared into the apartment, slamming the door behind him.

"Take the front," Detective Brightwell said to Officer Lomax. "I'll cover the back."

Officer Lomax ran down the driveway. Detective Brightwell pulled a gun from inside his jacket, and my heart dropped into my feet. He jumped the back steps in one leap and disappeared inside the apartment.

Sam started crying.

"What is the matter?" Angela asked.

"Uncle Ray is going to get a gun and shoot us," he sobbed. He grabbed my aching arm and hid his face in my T-shirt sleeve.

"No, he's not," I said. "We just searched his house,

Sam. I didn't see any guns. Did you?"

"No." He stopped crying and looked at me. "But he could have one in his pants."

I put my arm around him. "Even if he had a gun, I'm sure this car is bulletproof. Besides, the policemen will protect us."

Just then Officer Lomax came jogging down the alley, and Detective Brightwell reappeared at the back door of the bungalow.

"He's gone," Officer Lomax said, panting. "Neighbor kids said he ran east on Pico."

They got into the car. Detective Brightwell picked up the radio. He called Uncle Ray a *suspect* and asked for *units*.

"Apparently, you kids are right about your uncle. He was packing up his fire goodies, either to hide them or to use them again," Officer Lomax said.

Two more police cars pulled into the alley. Detective Brightwell got out and spoke to the officers. They searched Uncle Ray's trunk, then Detective Brightwell returned and said, "Let's get you kiddos home."

"What's going to happen to my uncle?" I asked.

"We'll get the warrant, search the house, and then probably arrest him," he said.

"If we can find him," Officer Lomax added dryly.

We drove down Pico Boulevard. "Are your parents home now?" Detective Brightwell asked.

"Umm . . . you can just drop us off here. We'll walk home," I said.

He laughed. "Nice try. The three of you are getting a police escort. Wouldn't want you to run into your uncle on your way home. He may be a little upset with you at the present moment."

"My parents are most probably at home," Angela said gloomily. She leaned back in her seat with resignation.

Mom is going to find out we went to Uncle Ray's, and she's going to be mad. But now we've got proof that Uncle Ray set the fire. Now the police will help us—finally.

When we pulled up to our apartment building, Detective Brightwell said he would speak to Mom. Officer Lomax walked Angela home.

"See you in about twenty years," Angela said over her shoulder.

Poor Angela. Mrs. V is going to freak when she sees the policeman. When he tells her what we did, her head will probably explode.

Sam and I led Detective Brightwell up to our apartment. He knocked and the door flew open.

"What's going on? Children, where have you been? You were supposed to come straight back from Mamac's. Who is this man? And where's Angela? Her mother's been calling and calling —"

"Detective Mark Brightwell, L.A.P.D.," the detective said, handing her his business card. "I called you this morning and notified you regarding the arson fire. Angela is back home now. It would be better if we could talk inside. May I come in?"

"Yes, come in." We crowded together in the living room. "Let's talk in the kitchen," Mom said awkwardly.

Sam and I sat across from Detective Brightwell at the kitchen table. Mom offered the detective lemonade, which he accepted. She set glasses for me and Sam but not for herself. The lemonade was tart and cold, and I gulped half the glass.

Detective Brightwell explained the events of the afternoon. Mom stared at me and Sam when he told her about us breaking into Uncle Ray's house.

They talked on and on, and my mind began to wander. *Mom is so pretty. Does she ever think about getting a boyfriend?*

Before he left, Detective Brightwell said, "Now, you kiddos stay out of trouble, and leave this to the police. If your uncle is involved, we'll handle it. Promise me you won't go climbing through any more windows."

"We promise," Sam and I said in unison.

"Jinx," Sam said.

I laughed. "Whatever, Sam." In spite of everything, a huge burden had been lifted from me. *The police will keep Mamac's house safe from now on.*

"I'll call you as soon as we know something," the detective said to Mom.

"Yes, please do, and thank you for bringing my children home."

Detective Brightwell smiled and backed out the front door, stumbling over the threshold as he went.

When the door was closed, I said, "He likes you."

"Oh you," Mom said, blushing. Then her face clouded. "You should not have gone to Ray's house."

"We had to get the *ebidence*," Sam said. "We knew it was him last night."

"What do you mean?" Mom asked suspiciously.

I stared at Sam with dagger eyes. "He means, we thought it was Uncle Ray who started the fire last night.

We were just talking about it."

"I should not have allowed you to go to Mamac's this morning. You are both to stay away from there and Ray's place until this is resolved. Promise me."

"I promise," I said.

"I promise too," Sam said.

"The good news is Mamac always paid her fire insurance premium. The insurance adjuster was already out there and assured me that the damage is fixable, and it's mostly covered by the policy. He even gave me the names of a few contractors. With a little luck, we'll still move in, right on schedule, in July."

"That's great, Mom," I said.

Mom gave us a big hug. "I don't want you kids to worry about this anymore." She squeezed us tight. "I couldn't bear it if anything happened to you."

Angela Slipping Away

Tap, tap, tap. I opened one eye and stared at my nightstand clock: five minutes before eight.

It's too early, my fuzzy brain told me. I struggled to my knees, slid the window open, and grabbed the lavender paper hanging on the line. Across the breezeway, Angela stood at her window. She waved. I pulled the note off the line and forced my sleepy eyes to read it.

Dear Thea,

My parents had a nervous breakdown when the policeman brought me home yesterday. Mother said I could have been murdered by your criminal uncle. I am grounded for 2 weeks!

Mother said you are a bad influence. She wants to take me to Boise.

My parents had a big fight. Mother said Father promised that our new house would be ready by now. She shouted, "You promised!"

Father shouted, "Get off my back!"

It is too dreadful!

❀ *Love, Angela* ❀

"What's wrong?" Sam's voice startled me. He lay motionless on his bed—dark eyes watching.

"Angela's grounded. I don't even know if she can be my friend anymore."

"'Cause of yesterday?"

"Of course."

"Sorry, Thea."

"Thanks."

I found Mom in the kitchen, drinking coffee and reading the Sunday paper.

"You're up early," she said. "I'll get breakfast started."

Mom hardly ever made dinner, but every Sunday she made pancakes, bacon, and scrambled eggs like Dad used to do. The smell of salty bacon and sweet pancakes reminded me of Dad standing at the stove, flipping pancakes in his old plaid bathrobe.

After Dad died, it didn't seem right that we should keep the Sunday breakfast tradition going. But Mom explained that she and Dad had been doing it since before Sam and I were born, and it made her happy. Now, two years without Dad, it had become *our* tradition.

Sam appeared in his pj's and plopped into a chair at the table.

"Good morning, honey," Mom said cheerfully. "Two early birds."

"I think I woke Sam up," I said. "Sorry, Sam."

"Angela sent Thea a note," Sam said. "She kept tapping on the window like she always does."

"I imagine her parents are very upset about yesterday," Mom said.

"They totally freaked out," I said. "Especially her mother. Why can't they just be normal—like you, Mom? I mean, you care, but you don't say, 'I must take drastic action,' over every little thing."

"I think that's a compliment, Thea. Thank you. I try not to 'freak-out' but what you three did yesterday was not a 'little thing.' If that's what you think—"

"I didn't mean that. I know we shouldn't have gone to Uncle Ray's, but Angela's mother freaks out about everything."

"What did Angela say in her note, if I may ask?" Mom said.

"She's grounded, and her mother wants to take her to Idaho, and she doesn't want us to be friends anymore."

"Oh dear," Mom said. She stopped mixing the pancake batter for a moment. "What a shame, honey. You girls are so close. Can't say I'm surprised though. Angela's parents are very conservative. What they must have thought when Angela arrived, escorted by a policeman. I'm glad I wasn't there to see it."

"Maybe they thought she was under arrest," Sam said.

I kicked him under the table. "I know it's hard, but could you try not to be a total dweeb this morning?"

"At first, I wasn't worried about you and Sam not coming straight back yesterday. I assumed you had gone to the park. But then, around eleven, Mrs. Vanderlin started calling. I didn't even know Angela was with you. Mrs. Vanderlin insisted that she was, and by noon, she was fit to be tied. She had called me five times!"

"Great," I said miserably.

"I drove over to Mamac's house to see if you were still there. I even checked inside the house. When I came out the front door, Mrs. Vanderlin's white Cadillac was blocking my car in the driveway. Can you imagine? Blocking my car! That woman—do you know what she said to me?"

"What?" Sam and I said in unison.

"Jinx," Sam said, laughing.

"Shush. What did she say, Mom?"

"She said, 'Mrs. MacRobert, we both know that you and I are not the same kind of people. My daughter would not even know Thea existed if it were not for the fact that our new domicile is not yet completed.'"

"She said that? She's such a—"

"What's a domy-style?" Sam asked.

"Domicile, hon. It means a house. Some people like to use fancy words every chance they get. She also said, 'I have come to see for myself if my daughter is here in this abandoned house.'"

"It's not abandoned," I mumbled.

"Then I said, 'You are a supercilious woman!'"

"Super-silliness?" Sam said.

"It means snobby," Mom explained. "Anyway, I said to her, 'I have no interest in hiding your daughter's whereabouts from you. If Angela doesn't confide in you, perhaps your mother-daughter relationship needs work. It has nothing to do with my family.'"

"Oh dang," I said.

"Don't worry, hon. As soon as I said that, I realized I did not want to sink to her level, so I said, 'We love Angela. Our daughters are friends because they enjoy each other's company. When I see Angela, I will call you.' That calmed her a bit. She said, 'Very well,' and drove off."

"I'm sorry, Mom. We really should have called."

Mom opened the kitchen cupboard and removed a jelly jar full of coins. I recognized it right away. It had been Dad's. He had kept it on his dresser and put spare change in it.

"See this jar, Thea? I don't want you to leave this apartment without taking a dime so you will always be able to call home."

"You give me an allowance. I don't need—"

"I know, but I've thought this over. It is our new rule. You always remember the front door key when you go out. Now, add a dime, and you're set. Check in—no excuses."

"Can I have a dime too, Mommy?" Sam asked.

"Yes, hon. When you go to Tim's, or out with your sister, you may take a dime too."

"Or, if I am outside in the dark, I can go to a phone booth, and call you, and tell you to come get me."

"Well, yes. But there is no reason for you to be outside in the dark," Mom said. "Speaking of Tim, Linda called. They're going to Yosemite for two weeks. So, for the next two weeks, you won't be able to stay with Tim while I'm at work. I'd like you to stay with your sister, but I need you two to stay out of trouble. What do you say, Thea?"

The more time Sam's with me, the more time I'll have to work on him so he won't blab to mom.

"Hey, what makes you think I want to stay with her?" Sam asked.

"Do you?" Mom asked.

"I guess so," Sam said.

He just can't admit that he loves to hang out with me, I thought. "Fine," I said as if I didn't care one way or the other.

*T*he next day was Monday. After Mom left for work, Sam and I went for a bike ride.

"Got your inhaler?" I asked as we headed out the door.

"Holy guacamole, Thea! You don't have to remind me all the time. I can take care of myself."

"Okay, okay."

At the carport, we unlocked our bikes. "Let's go to the willow tree!" Sam said.

"No way, Sam. Mom would kill us if we went to Mamac's now."

"We won't tell her."

"Do you want to run into Uncle Ray? How do you know he's not hiding in the backyard?"

That shut him up. We spent the rest of the day riding our bikes and playing cards.

On Tuesday, we decided to go to Mar Vista Pool. It was one o'clock by the time we packed our stuff and got on our bikes. It was hot, and the pool was crowded.

"Meet you at the deep end," I said to Sam in front of the dressing rooms. It took me longer than Sam to put my suit on, and when I came out, I had to hunt for him through the bunches of noisy children and lounging teenagers. I found him near the fence at the deep end.

"I'm going in," Sam said.

"Sure, go ahead," I said.

Sam trotted off, and I sat on my towel and opened my canvas bag. I pulled out my copy of *Teen Beat* magazine and set it beside me. Then I leaned back on my hands and looked around at the crowd.

I was about to pick up my magazine when, across the pool, a blonde girl in a paisley-print two-piece caught my eye. She shook out her towel and laid it on the cement. Next to her stood a slender girl in a bright red bikini. Her brown hair was pulled back in a tight ponytail.

Jessica and Angela? That can't be. Angela's grounded. The blonde girl turned and knelt on her towel. *That is Angela!* To their right, two women lay on chaise longues. Slim and tanned, they wore oversized sunglasses and wide-brimmed hats. *That's Mrs. V! That must be Jessica's mother with her. I guess Angela's not really grounded. She's just grounded from being with me.*

Jessica and Angela sat side-by-side on their towels. Jessica started rummaging through a bag, then she held up a handful of brightly colored bottles.

"Nail polish," I whispered out loud. The two girls laughed and passed the bottles back and forth. Then they each picked a bottle and got busy painting their toenails.

A wet body blocked the sun. "Don't you want to go in?" Sam asked, dripping and shivering.

"No."

Sam knelt on his towel.

I lay on my stomach and buried my face in my arms.

"What's wrong?" Sam asked.

"Angela's here with Jessica," I said into my towel.

"Where?" Sam said, looking around.

"Don't look over there. They'll see us," I said.

"So?"

"I'm so embarrassed."

"Why?"

"Forget it," I said.

Sam lay on his back. After he was good and hot, he went back in the pool. I peered out, resting my chin on the back of my hand. Angela's and Jessica's moms were still reclined on their chaise longues, but Angela and Jessica weren't with them. I scanned the crowd—there, in the snack line, paisley and red. Jessica was laughing and talking to some kids. She put her hand on a boy's shoulder. Ricky!

Balancing food and paper cups, Angela and Jessica followed Ricky and two other boys to a round table with an umbrella. The five of them sat, eating and laughing. *Angela looks so happy.*

After they ate, they swam and horsed around in the pool. They even played chicken. Jessica sat on the shoulders of one of the boys, and Angela sat on Ricky's shoulders as they batted and pulled, trying to topple each other.

I cradled my head in my arms and burst into tears. *I should be happy for Angela. She's crazy about Ricky. Jessica is setting them up—just like she promised. Why be friends with me? I have a criminal uncle. I have a dad who was killed. We didn't really see Mamac above the willow tree. That was just a dream. Of course she wasn't there when we went back with Sam. That's because she's dead. Dead! As in, gone forever.*

I fell asleep. When I woke up, Angela and Jessica were gone, and so were their moms. I swam a little, then Sam and I went home.

*E*very night when I went to sleep, I wondered if I would dream about the willow tree. Every day, I went to my dresser, opened my heart-box, and looked at my cameo treasure. Sometimes I held the brooch in the palm of my hand. That made me feel like Mamac was in the next room and had just given me a big hug. I never held the cameo when I went to sleep though. I figured, if Mamac wanted me to have the dream again, it would happen without the cameo.

The following Tuesday, a week after I saw Angela and Jessica at the swimming pool, Detective Brightwell called Mom. He told her the police had searched Uncle Ray's apartment. In a cupboard, they found a black duffel bag that smelled of gasoline. Inside, there was a flashlight. They already had the rags, newspapers, and gas can that Uncle Ray had left in the trunk of his car the day he ran from the police. It was all evidence. Now they just needed to find Uncle Ray so they could arrest him.

Meanwhile, Mamac's house was being fixed. On

Wednesday evening, we went with Mom to check on the progress. "Detective Brightwell is meeting us there," Mom said.

We pulled into Mamac's driveway at seven o'clock. The construction workers had quit for the day, but it was still light out. Mom said, "I guess Detective Brightwell hasn't arrived yet."

"Can we wait in the car?" I asked. "Uncle Ray might be here."

"We could, but we're not going to. I'm not going to spend my life jumping at shadows. We have a right to be here, and we're not going to hide. Besides, the detective will be here any second," she added, opening the car door.

I scanned the front yard as I followed Mom and Sam up the drive. The lawn needed mowing, and all the window shades were closed. *Looks different now—different without Mamac.*

"Look at that," Mom said. "They've already scraped away the burnt part and have applied fresh white stucco."

"Looks like a puzzle," Sam said, eyeing the white splotches on the pink stucco. He hopped on a ladder left leaning against the house and peered through a window. "Hey, where'd the furniture go? And how come the floor's bumpy?"

"The workmen moved the furniture. The floor is bumpy because it's warped," Mom said. "When the fire department put out the fire they soaked the hardwood floors. They will be refinished later this week."

The gate latch rattled, and my heart went *thump, thump, thump.*

"There you are." It was Detective Brightwell. He

laughed. There was nothing funny. He just looked happy to see us.

"Come on, Sam," I said. "Let's find a broom and sweep the driveway." Sam came down the ladder, and I led him away.

Mom and Detective Brightwell stood by the gate and talked while Sam and I swept the sawdust and tidied the wood scraps left by the workers.

After a bit, Mom called, "Kids, Mark has invited us out for pizza. Would you like that?"

"Who's Mark?" Sam asked.

"I mean, Detective Brightwell," Mom stammered.

"Okay," I said. Sam didn't say anything.

Mark followed us to Shakey's Pizza Parlor in his red Fiat convertible. We ordered mushroom and olive pizza. Mom and Mark joked and laughed the whole time we were eating. As soon as I was finished, I grabbed Sam's hand, and we wandered off to watch the player piano that stood next to the huge fireplace where a gas fire burned. The warmth from the fire felt good on my arms and face.

Sam stood watching the piano keys move, seemingly by an invisible hand. "Magic," he said.

"What? No, Sam. Dad explained it to me once. Air goes through holes in the paper and moves levers that make the keys go. There's no such thing as magic."

Sam's mouth was set in a firm, upside down smile.

"What's the matter?"

"I don't like that policeman," Sam said.

"I think he's nice."

"I like it just the three of us."

"Sam, the detective likes Mom. That's a good thing."

When we went back to our table, Mark said, "I almost forgot—a friend of mine at the fire department gave me these. The perfect present for you two."

He reached into the pocket of his leather jacket and pulled out two small silver objects. He dropped one into each of our palms. They were identical, miniature silver fire hydrants.

"They have the fire department's phone number on them in case you need to report a fire," he said. His blue-gray eyes fell on me, watching.

"Thanks," I muttered. I stared across the room at the fire in the fireplace. It danced happily, but I felt miserable. *I was trying to do the right thing when I reported the fire. It WAS the right thing. But then I lied about it. Did I lie? I just didn't tell the whole story. That's the same as lying.*

"Cool," Sam said.

"That's very sweet," Mom said.

Mom and Sam don't have any idea why he's giving us these. He knows it was me who reported the fire. He's a detective. He can tell when a person isn't telling the truth. He's going to keep after me until I tell him. But I can't tell him. I can't ever tell him . . . .

We left the restaurant. Out in the parking lot, Mark said, "Good night, kiddos." He turned to Mom. "Can I call you tomorrow, Michelle?"

"Yes, I'd like that," Mom said.

When we were back in our car, Sam said, "Mommy, are you going to marry him?"

"Don't be silly," Mom said, but she was smiling.

It was ten o'clock by the time we arrived home.

"Time for bed," Mom said. "I have to get up early for

work."

I brushed my teeth and went to my bedroom. Sam was already asleep. *Nice to be the little brother and not have to worry about everything. I have so much to think about.*

I turned out the light on my nightstand and settled into my comfy bed. Pictures skipped through my head like clips from a movie: the three of us living in Mamac's house, Mom making spaghetti, eating at the big maple table, the willow tree . . . crooked branches, sweeping leaves . . .

I was half-dreaming, half-awake, when I heard, t*ap, tap, tap.*

Must have been outside somewhere . . . I settled back into my pillow.

It came again—still faint, but faster now, k*nock, knock, knock.* Then louder, insistent, *THUMP, THUMP, THUMP.*

A Late-Night Visitor

$\mathcal{M}$y eyes flew open. The room was dark. I checked the clock—two minutes before eleven. *What's going on?* I slipped out of bed, peeked out the door, and crept down the hall to the living room.

Mom was standing at the front door in her long blue robe. The nightlight on the mail table made her silhouette tall and weirdly skinny on the wall behind her. She leaned forward and peeked through the peephole then jumped back as if it had bitten her.

"I'm calling the police if you don't leave here immediately," she whispered forcefully through the locked door. She started fumbling with papers on the mail table, searching for Detective Brightwell's business card. Bills scattered and dropped to the floor.

"Michelle, please," a muffled voice begged. "I have to talk to you. It's about Howie—I want to tell you . . . ."

At the mention of my father's name, Mom dropped the

papers in her hand. She stood still as a statue, then she reached for the doorknob.

"Mom, don't let him in!"

"I'm not afraid," she said. Her voice sounded strange, and she didn't look at me. "I've been waiting a long time to hear what he has to say about Howard."

"Are you sober?" she asked.

"Cold sober," the muffled voice replied.

Mom flipped the lock and opened the door. Uncle Ray's tall figure filled the shadowy landing.

"Can I come in?"

Mom led my uncle into the kitchen and insisted on making him hot tea. I sat across from him and marveled at my mother's kindness. *After all the bad stuff Uncle Ray has done, she wants to serve him tea?* I eyed my uncle warily, ready to jump to Mom's defense if he made a wrong move.

But Uncle Ray didn't look dangerous. His eyes were red, and his plaid shirt was wrinkled and buttoned wrong.

The teakettle whistled. Mom dropped a tea bag into a heavy green mug, filled it with steaming water, and set it before Uncle Ray.

Uncle Ray wrapped his hands around the mug as if to warm them. "I've been hiding for days. Is there a warrant for my arrest?"

"Yes, there is. You should turn yourself in. What do you want to tell me about Howard?"

Uncle Ray took a deep breath. "Michelle, I have to come clean with you. I've kept this lousy secret for two years. You deserve the truth. You always deserved the truth." He paused. "I was there when Howie was shot."

Mom stared at my uncle. "I figured as much," she said.

"It was an accident. A terrible accident that took my brother's life, and wrecked your life, and your kids' lives. Howie's death wrecked my life too. I loved my big brother." Uncle Ray's voice cracked, and he began to sob.

Mom handed him a paper napkin to wipe his face. "Ray, what happened?" she prodded.

"The day Howie died, I went to see him with Bruno Garner. I was desperate to come up with two thousand dollars to pay these bookies who had been running a tab for me. I was heavy into betting back then—races, sports, cards. Anyway, I was on a bad losing streak. Bruno told me that if I didn't give him two grand, he and his buddies were going to get me. You know, break my legs, or whatever those guys do—even kill me." He looked at Mom as if he were expecting something—sympathy?

"Go on," Mom said.

"I didn't know what to do, so I called Howie. He told me to come over. I told him Bruno was with me, but he said come over anyway. He said he would talk to Bruno—set up a payment plan or something. That was just like Howie—always trying to help—no matter how big a mess I was in." Uncle Ray stared at his cup then took a sip of the steaming tea.

"Continue," Mom said.

"When we arrived, Howie led us into the living room. He was talking real nice to Bruno—trying to convince him to compromise about the money. Bruno just laughed. He said, 'Pay up for your little brother or he's gonna get it.' Howie said he didn't have two thousand dollars. Bruno pulled out a gun and pointed it at me. He said, 'Let's go.' I started toward the front door. Howie grabbed Bruno's arm. He was trying to save me . . . ."

Uncle Ray started crying again. Tears ran into the wrinkled crevices around his eyes. He wiped his nose with the napkin and sniffed.

"I'm not sure how it happened. They were wrestling. The gun went off. Howie fell backward onto the floor. Bruno ran out the front door. He took his gun with him. I ran to Howie. It was over. He was hit in the chest. He was dead. I just sat there in a daze. Then I heard a siren. Someone must have heard the gunshot and called the cops, so I got up and ran away."

"How could you leave your brother like that—shot down, helpless?"

"I was scared. I was on parole. The judge had warned me, 'Any more trouble—you're going back to prison.' Later on, when the cops questioned me about Howie, I said, 'I don't know anything about it.' There was nothing to lead them to me or Bruno. When Howie let us in, he left the front door open. So when Bruno and I left, we didn't leave fingerprints on the doorknob."

As I listened to Uncle Ray, I felt like a spring as big as my fist was being wound in my chest—tighter and tighter—until it was so tight, it exploded.

"Dad is dead because of you!" I shouted. "You could have told us what happened a long time ago, but you left us wondering and not knowing. You are the meanest man in the whole world! I wish you were dead instead of Dad."

I started sobbing. I didn't want to, especially in front of Uncle Ray, but I couldn't help it, and I couldn't stop. My heart hurt. I just wanted my dad so much, and at that moment—after listening to Mom and Uncle Ray talking about what happened to him like a story from long ago—the truth hit me in a new way. Dad wasn't just gone. He was never coming back. Never.

"I don't blame you for hating me," Uncle Ray said. "I wish it had been me instead of him too."

Mom sat down next to me and put her arm around me. "What's happening now, Ray?" she asked.

"After Howie was shot, I didn't hear from Bruno. I thought I was done with him. But somehow, he found out about Mamac passing away. He must have figured I would inherit money. He popped up out of nowhere and said, I don't owe him two thousand dollars, now I owe him twenty thousand! Two thousand, plus eight thousand in interest, plus another ten thousand for all the trouble he says I caused him with my brother. He said if I don't give him the money, he'll testify against me in court and say I shot Howie because he wouldn't give me money to bet the horse races.

"Michelle, I felt so bad about what happened. I promised Bruno the ten thousand from Mamac's life insurance. He said if I gave him ten thousand more, he'd go away, and I'd never hear from him again. He gave me two weeks to get the money."

"And the fire, that was you?" Mom asked.

"Yeah, that was me. When I found out I'd have to wait ten years to get Mamac's house, I started feeling sorry for myself. I had this idea that if I burned the house, I could collect the fire insurance money. I took my gas can and went over there the other night. I also took a bottle of Jack Daniel's whiskey with me. By the time I lit the fire, I was wasted. I sat there like an idiot, crying and watching the house burn. Then I heard the sirens. That sobered me up. I thought about staying so I'd get caught. But at the last second, I ran through the backyard and jumped the fence. I am such a coward, Michelle."

"Yes, you are," Mom agreed. "And you can run out of here and continue to be one, or you can do the right thing for once in your wretched life and turn yourself in."

"That's what I came to tell you. I'm going to turn myself in. I wanted to tell you the truth first. I figured I could at least give you that."

Uncle Ray finished his tea. Then he called the police. It took them over an hour to arrive. Even though I hated Uncle Ray that night, it was hard to watch the police handcuff him and lead him away.

$\mathcal{T}$he next night, Angela called. "I can only speak for a few minutes," she said.

"What have you been doing?"

"Oh, the usual, shopping with Mother—furniture hunting mostly—for the new house."

"So, you're not grounded?"

"I go out with Mother."

"I saw you, Angela."

"You did?"

"Yes, with Jessica at the pool."

"Umm . . . you know our mothers are friends. We tagged along with them. Mother wanted to work on her tan. Jessica and I had fun. I told you she is nice." She giggled, remembering some silliness they had shared.

"Your mother doesn't want us to be friends anymore?"

"I still want to be friends, but Mother was hysterical after the policeman brought me home."

"Oh," I said.

"It is not all your fault. I wanted to go to your uncle's house too. Oh my goodness. I want to tell you—Mother saw the police take your uncle away last night. She said his hands were handcuffed behind his back."

"She saw that?"

"There was a police car in the alley. The flashing red light woke her up. She watched from the window."

My face burned with shame, imagining Mrs. V watching Uncle Ray being put in a police car.

"Mother says that since we are moving to the Valley soon, I should start broadening my horizons. You know, mixing with new people."

Better people, you mean, I thought. "Are you still going to Boise for the rest of summer?"

"I am not sure. Father says it is too expensive to fly."

"Who are you talking to?" It was Mrs. V.

"I am talking to Jessica. I have to go now, Jessica. Goodbye."

I thought about Angela every day, hoping she wouldn't leave for Idaho and wanting us to go back to being best friends.

I also thought about moving to Mamac's. I was jazzed that I was going to have my own bedroom again—Mamac's sewing room on the back corner of the house. From the window, I could see the garden and the brick path that leads to the willow tree.

On Saturday, Mom, Sam, and I went to Mamac's. I took down the pink-rosebud curtains that hung in my new bedroom to wash them. On my way to the back porch where the washing machine was located, I ran into Mom.

"Thea, would you like me to replace those curtains? We could go to Sears and pick out something pretty," she said.

"No, Mom," I said, hugging the yards of faded cotton. "I like these. They smell smoky. I'll wash them."

I loaded the curtains into Mamac's pink washing machine and set the dial to *Delicate*. *I remember playing under the sewing machine when Mamac made these—it was raining pink rosebuds all around me. The sewing machine motor went chug, chug, chug . . . .*

Mamac's house was full of thirty years of stuff. When it came time to decide what to do with her pink refrigerator, Mom said, "We don't own the one in our apartment. This pink one is a little small. We could buy—"

"Mommy, we have to keep it," Sam said.

"Why is that, hon?" Mom asked.

"Because it's where Mamac kept all her good food."

"I see. We better keep it then. At least for now."

Mom filled box after box with books and knickknacks. Once, I found her kneeling on the floor holding a photo album. She ran her fingertips over a black-and-white photo of Dad as a young man. Her eyes glistened, and her lips moved as if she were speaking, but she didn't say anything.

Sometimes she'd say, "We'll save this for Ray." Then she'd write *Ray* on a box and set it on the stack to be stored in the attic.

One night, Sam was with us in the living room. He was supposed to be washing the windows, but it looked to me like he was smearing the dirt around with too many paper towels.

"And this box—for Ray," Mom said.

"For Uncle Ray?" Sam asked. "He's bad."

Mom stopped what she was doing and looked at Sam. "Honey, Ray did some bad things, but he's not a bad person." She went back to packing old books in the cardboard box in front of her. "The things in this house belonged to Ray's mother and father, and some of these old books were his when he was little. Maybe someday he'll get his life together and want them."

"But he's in jail now, right?" I asked.

"He's out on bail. His hearing is in a few days. The judge ordered him not to come near this house or any of us, and your uncle has promised not to bother us."

*F*inally, our new home was ready. The broken windows had been replaced, and Mamac's oak floors were refinished and glowed with golden warmth. The pink walls were now white, and the windows, in spite of Sam, were sparkling clean. *Tomorrow we get to move in! And, starting tomorrow, Angela won't be grounded!*

Angela had sent me a note on the pulley, saying she could come over tomorrow. I wrote her back and told her it was our moving day, and she said she would help. *We can stay friends after all. I can hardly wait to see her!*

But that evening, while I was in my bedroom trying to get the clothes in my closet to hang on separate hangers, Mom popped in and said, "Thea, Angela is on the phone."

"Thea, you will never guess! We are going to Hawaii!"

"Cool," I said. Jealousy and disappointment dumped

on me like a bucket of cold spaghetti.

"My grandparents, and my uncle, and two aunts, plus my cousins, are going to rent a house right on the beach. Mother bought the airline tickets today. We depart Sunday morning! I am so excited!"

"Groovy," I said.

"I will miss you," Angela said.

"How long will you be gone?"

"Two months, I think. A week in Hawaii and then off to Boise. Mother convinced Father that she would go mad staying here all summer. We must be back in time for me to start school in the Valley. Father has promised our house will be ready by then."

"Is he going to Hawaii too?"

Angela lowered her voice. "No. I think he is glad we are going so he can have peace. They have been quarreling a lot. Tomorrow, I have to go shopping for the trip, so I am unable to help you move. Sorry, Thea."

"That's okay," I said, my heart sinking.

"Mother promised we will stop at Mamac's, I mean your new house, tomorrow night, to say goodbye. All right?"

"Okay. Come over tomorrow night." I hung up the phone and sat on Mom's bed, staring at nothing.

The next day, I worked harder than I had in my entire life. Mark came over with his best friend, who turned out to be Mario Lomax, the police officer who had driven us home two weeks before. They had rented a small U-Haul truck.

"Hello, beautiful people," Mark said. His frame filled the front doorway, and the top of his head almost touched the top of the doorjamb. He looked around at the open cupboards and stacks of boxes and bags and his smiling eyes twinkled with mischief.

"Michelle, I hate to tell you this, but your belongings have escaped and left a trail of anarchy and mayhem in their wake," he said.

Mom laughed. "Good thing I have two commandos to squelch the revolution."

Mark and Mario moved the couch, beds, and dressers. Sam and I carried boxes and piles of clothes to the truck. When we arrived at our new house, we helped unload them too. Each box had a room designation written on it: *kitchen, living room, bathroom,* and for the three bedrooms: *Sam, Thea,* or *Mom.*

We made the move in two trips. By dinnertime, we were beat. Mom ordered two giant mushroom-and-olive pizzas and five large Cokes from Pizza Man. When the food arrived, we gathered around Mamac's big maple table in the breakfast room.

As the grown-ups talked and laughed, I gazed out the window at the garden—a thousand shades of green, intensified by the yellow rays from the summer sun, shimmered in the last hour of light.

The dichondra was a blue-green sea that swept the yard. Where the brick path turned, the Queen Elizabeth roses stood in their brick-bordered bed—tall green stalks, adorned with fluffy pink crowns. To the right, the lemon tree—really an oversized lemon bush—was loaded with yellow fruit. The soldier hedge, with its purple poison-plums, was dressed in shiny black-green leaves and stood guard along the fence line. In the far left corner, forming the backdrop of this oasis, grew the enormous weeping willow. Its long, slender, gray-green tendrils danced invitingly in the gentle breeze. My eyes settled just above the willow, and I imagined the invisible staircase and my beautiful Mamac standing on it.

Out of the corner of my eye, I noticed Sam was also staring out the window. Then three pairs of adult eyes fixed on us.

"Hey, you two, is a UFO landing in the yard?" Mario Lomax joked.

"Did you see her?" Sam asked.

"See who?" Mario asked.

"Mamac."

"What?" Mom looked startled.

I kicked Sam under the table. "He's kidding," I said.

Sam fell silent and stared at his pizza.

Angela came at eight thirty. Mark and Mario had just left. Mrs. V waited outside in her white Cadillac—engine running, lights on.

"I cannot stay long," Angela said as she burst in the front door. Her cheeks shone pink, and her eyes had an excited, faraway sparkle. She gave me a big hug. "Goodbye, Thea. Have a wonderful summer."

"Goodbye," I said. I felt like a six-hundred-pound gorilla was sitting on my chest.

"Goodbye, Mrs. MacRobert." Angela hugged Mom.

"Have a great time in Hawaii and Idaho. We'll be thinking of you," Mom said.

"Farewell, Samuel," Angela said. Sam backed away, but Angela grabbed his shoulders and hugged him. "Stay out of trouble, little friend."

"You should talk," Sam said, shaking her off.

A few more seconds and Angela was out the door. Her golden hair swung cheerfully as she hurried down the walkway. She climbed into the Cadillac and had to climb halfway out again to pull the big door shut. The car pulled into the street. Its red taillights were visible for three blocks, then the turn signal blinked red, and Angela disappeared around the corner and into the night.

The Fall

Working on our new home helped distract me from missing Angela every second of the day. We still had to arrange the furniture, and there was tons of unpacking to do. I loved my new bedroom. Mom bought me a duvet to cover my old comforter. It was covered with pink rosebuds and almost perfectly matched the rosebud curtains Mamac had made.

As soon as my dresser was positioned along the wall and the drawers were put back where they belonged, I slid open the top drawer and dug under a pile of socks for my silver heart-box. I wiggled the lid off and was glad to see my precious cameo resting inside. Gingerly, I slid it into my palm. Then I wandered over to the window to examine it in the light.

The profiled face of the cameo lady was smooth like poured cream. Her nose was straight, and her hair was piled in a neat roll around her face. Her mouth—*I never noticed that—she's smiling.* I smiled too. Then I said a prayer:

> *Dear Mamac,*
> *I hope you are happy in heaven. We are all fine here. I miss you a lot. Thank you for this beautiful cameo, and thank you for letting us live in your house.*
> *Amen.*

I hadn't been up the willow tree since the night Uncle Ray set the fire. Angela had been grounded, so I couldn't go with her. I hadn't wanted to sneak over with Sam because I had told him the invisible staircase wasn't real. I could have gone alone, but I was afraid to sneak out in the dark by myself.

Now that we were in our new house, every morning Sam asked, "Thea, can we climb the willow today?"

"Not today," I would say. "Let's do it tomorrow."

After five days of this, Sam declared, "I'm gonna climb it without you."

"You can't go without me."

"Then you come too. Why don't you want to?"

"I don't want to because—I told you before, there's no reason to—that was just a game."

"I know, but I want to anyway—like before, after school."

We could go up one last time . . . . If the staircase isn't there, maybe Sam will stop asking. I just don't want him to tell Mom we snuck over here at night. She'd never trust me again. Oh crap! Total catastrophe: Sam tells Mom—Mom tells Mark. Mark is already halfway sure I was the one who reported the fire. If Sam tells on us, Mark would know it was me. Mark is nice, but he's a detective. He would put it in his report. The whole police department would know. They'd contact Angela's parents. We'd be in huge, never-ending trouble.

"Okay, Sam. We'll climb it on Saturday. But not because we are looking for anything special. We'll climb it because we used to after school."

On Saturday, Mom said she was going out for dinner with Mark. "We'll be at the Pelican's Catch on Malibu Pier. Their number is on the fridge. Be good, you two. I'll be back by ten."

Sam and I stood at the window watching Mom and Mark walk toward Mark's spiffy, red Fiat. He opened the passenger door and made a sweeping gesture with his arm as if Mom were a great lady and he were her coachman. Mom laughed and got in. They backed out of the driveway, and Mom's hair blew in the wind as they whizzed down the street.

"Cool car," Sam said.

"Looks like one of your matchbox cars," I said.

"That's what I was thinking. *¡Vámonos!*" Sam grabbed my arm and pulled me toward the back door.

It was almost dusk when we stepped into the backyard. A Santa Ana breeze warmed the air and ruffled the leaves of every bush and shrub. We headed down the brick path and rounded the back of the garage. The slender leaves of the willow tree flittered as if to say, *hello.*

It's only the wind.

Sam skipped ahead—across the dichondra to the willow. "Me first," he called, disappearing behind the drooping branches.

When I caught up, he was already in the tree. *Is the invisible staircase waiting for us?* I shivered.

I pulled myself up into the nook where the main branches forked. Sam was halfway up the left side. He didn't stop climbing until he was directly below where the invisible staircase had been. I climbed higher and put my arm around the trunk for security as I watched him.

Just as I had done a few weeks before, Sam placed one foot in front of the other as he reached into the air above his head, searching.

"Doggone it! I can't reach," he said. He did the tightrope walk in reverse, back to the trunk. He grabbed the branch above his head and swung up onto it as if it were a monkey bar.

"We never went on that branch. It's too skinny," I said.

"Too skinny for two fat girls but not for me."

"Come down—right now!"

Sam was straddling the thin branch and began inching forward.

CRACK! The sound was unmistakable—dry wood snapping. Sam let out a yelp.

Time slowed—like a molasses-covered nightmare—as I watched my brother drop, hit a branch, turn slightly, then fall sideways. The leaves shook, and the branches quivered. Then it all stopped. Sam was a dark, motionless heap on the ground, far below.

"Sam!" I screamed.

He didn't move. He didn't answer.

I couldn't think. I slid down the branches, scraping my arms and legs as I went. My foot slipped, and I almost fell backward. *Careful. Don't you fall too!* I swung onto the main fork of the trunk and jumped to the hard dirt below. Leaves and sticks littered the ground, and I stumbled as I ran to Sam.

"Sam, are you okay? Sam, say something."

Sam's eyes were shut. He looked like he was sleeping, except one arm was bent behind his back.

"Sam, wake up! Please, wake up! Sam, speak to me!"

"Thea . . ." his voice was a whisper. "I fell." His eyes were still closed.

"I'm going for help. Don't move."

"My arm—"

"I'm going to call Mom. I'll be right back."

I raced across the lawn and up the brick path. I leapt the steps to the back door and stormed the kitchen. I grabbed the pink phone on the counter, then I froze. *What did Mom say? Restaurant—Malibu Pier—on the fridge.*

The refrigerator door was covered with takeout menus, photos, kids' drawings, and grocery lists. Everything was on the fridge!

My hands were shaking as I pushed them about. Magnets began sliding. Some clattered to the floor. Photos and artwork went everywhere. Some sailed lazily across the kitchen.

"Where is it?" I shouted. My mind was filled with Sam lying under the tree, his arm twisted in that wrong way. *He might even be dying out there—alone.*

The house was dusky. I felt along the wall and flipped the light switch. A torn sheet of paper was sticking out from under my foot.

Pelican's Catch (213) 555-4550

I recognized Mom's handwriting. I grabbed the phone again and headed out the back door. The cord only reached as far as the back steps, and I couldn't see Sam from there. I knelt on the landing and started dialing. My finger slipped off the rotary dial halfway through the third number, and I had to hang up and start again.

Ring, ring—background noise—a woman's voice, "Pelican's Catch. Reservations required. How may I help you this evening?"

"I need to speak to my mom. She's eating dinner there. Her name is Michelle MacRobert."

"One moment, please." She put me on hold.

A man's voice this time, "Pelican's Catch. Reservations required. How may I help you this evening?"

"I told that other lady that I need to talk to my mom. Her name is Michelle MacRobert. Could you please find her?"

"I'm checking. What time was her reservation?"

"I don't know."

"Sorry, deary. I must have—"

"Mark Brightwell! Look for Mark Brightwell."

"And, you are . . . ?"

"Mark Brightwell is a policeman. If you don't get my mom right now, you're gonna be in big—"

Click. I was on hold, again!

"Hey Jude," a song by the Beatles, started playing.

And don't you know that it's just you,
Hey, Jude, you'll do.
The movement you need is on your shoulder.
Nah nah nah—

Click—more background noise. "Thea?"

"Mom! Sam fell out of the tree."

"Oh, dear God! Is he all right?"

"I don't know. He's lying on the ground."

"Is he conscious? I mean, is he awake?"

"Sort of. He spoke a little."

"I'm going to call an ambulance. Don't let him move. Stay with him. Wait—what? Mark says do not let him fall asleep. Keep him warm and quiet and awake. We're on our way."

"Okay."

I ran back to the willow tree and dropped to my knees by Sam's side.

"Sam, Mom's coming. Just lay still."

Sam's eyes were shut, and his face was deathly white in the fading light. "I'm cold," he whispered.

I whipped off my sweatshirt and gently laid it over him.

"Thea . . ."

I lay on my side, my face close to Sam's. His eyes blinked open. *Dad's eyes.*

"I'm right here, Sam."

"Remember when we flew, and we were on top of the clock tower?"

"Yeah . . ." Guilt gurgled inside me, and I tried to fix the lie I had told my brother. "Sam, about that night—it wasn't right that I told you it didn't really happen—"

"You flew away, and me and Angela went to our old house where we lived with Mommy and Daddy. It was hard to find. Looks different when you're high up."

"Kind of dumb of me to think you would believe— Wait a minute! What did you say? You went to our old house with Angela?"

"The tree in front with the sticky purple flowers—I couldn't tell if they were purple in the dark—so I picked one, and it was sticky."

"It's called a jacaranda tree. Those sticky flowers used to drop on Dad's car. He'd get mad about it."

"Our playhouse is still there—in the backyard."

"Really?"

"When we lived in our apartment, Mommy and I drove to our old house sometimes on the way back from the grocery store."

"You did?"

"Yeah. Mommy likes to do that."

"I didn't know that," I said.

"Angela and me saw a swing set and a little pool in the backyard too. Who are those people living in our house?"

"I don't know—a family, I guess."

"Does a little boy live there?"

"Sure, probably."

"Does he sleep in my room?"

"He could."

"I hope he likes it. I hope he likes my room."

"Me too," I said. Carefully, I pushed back the strands of hair that had fallen over Sam's eyes. "We have a nice house now too."

"I like it here," Sam said. "But it's different now. Mamac's not here."

"She's still here in a way. I mean—in my mind—I imagine her washing dishes or cooking something good on the stove. Remember how she'd stir the fudge then dump it on the wax paper at exactly the right second before it got too hard?"

We lay there for a few seconds, not talking. I heard a siren. It was getting louder.

"I'm never telling anyone what we did. I didn't even tell Tim," Sam said.

"I know you won't tell. Besides, Angela and I told you it never happened." I laughed, trying to make a joke of it.

"Right. It didn't happen," Sam said.

The siren stopped. I jumped up and peeked through the curtain of willow leaves. Two paramedics came running toward us. They carried a stretcher and a black bag with a red cross on it.

"Here we are," I called.

"Hey, bud. How you doing?" the taller paramedic asked as he knelt beside Sam.

"I fell," Sam whispered.

They put a neck brace on him and rolled him onto his back. He moaned. When they put the splint on his arm, he cried out. I felt nauseous as I watched them work on my little brother. They covered him with a blanket and lifted him onto the stretcher. The tall paramedic spoke in a calm, friendly voice the whole time.

"You're doing great, Sam. Lucky for you, your big sister was here to call for help."

They carried Sam to the front of the house. They were putting him into the back of the ambulance when Mom and Mark drove up. Mom jumped out of Mark's car and ran over to us.

"How is he?" she asked.

"They'll check him out from head to toe at the hospital," the shorter paramedic said.

"I'm riding with you," Mom said. She climbed into the back of the ambulance without waiting for permission.

"We'll follow in my car," Mark said. I had never ridden in a convertible. It would have been fun if I hadn't been worried about Sam.

When we reached the hospital, the ambulance disappeared into the *Ambulance Only* entrance. Mark parked in a nearby lot, and we found our way to the emergency room. *St. John's Hospital. This is where Mamac died. I hate this place.*

A nurse appeared. "You must be Thea, and you are Detective Brightwell? Mrs. MacRobert asked me to fill you in. Sam is in x-ray now. We'll know more after the radiologist has reviewed his pictures. There's not much room back there, and it would be best if you two could wait out here. Shouldn't be too long."

Mark and I sat. The waiting room was empty except for an old woman with two small children who sat across from us.

"Sorry, kiddo," Mark said.

"For what?"

"For taking your mom out tonight. I realize now that we should have stayed home. We could have made dinner with you and Sam."

"We always climb that tree," I said. "If Sam would have listened to me and not climbed so high—"

"Thea, you know I was baiting you when I gave you and Sam those silver fire hydrants at Shakey's Pizza Parlor, right?"

"Baiting me?"

"Yes, I wanted to see what you'd do—just seeing your

expression was enough."

"Enough? What do you mean?"

"I know you were the 'child, probably female,' who called the fire department the night of the fire."

"Oh?" I said, staring straight ahead.

"Believe it or not, I'm a good detective, and that means I'm very skilled at reading people. I was a kid once—it was about a hundred years ago—but I remember the daring things we did. Maybe the three of you thought it would be fun to go to your grandmother's house in the dark, and by sheer coincidence, stumbled upon your uncle making mischief in the driveway. In any case, I'm convinced you had nothing to do with setting the fire. You called the fire department, and as you pointed out at the station, that was a good thing. Who reported the fire is not part of the arson investigation. We know who set the fire, and that's what matters."

I stared at Mark. This was the second time he had taken a huge weight off my shoulders. "Okay," I said.

"I think you and Sam are great kids. I don't know what you think of me, but I like your mom a lot. I've never been married. Some people would tell you I'm married to my job, but I do hope to marry someday—"

Just then Mom came through the swinging door. I jumped to my feet.

"What's his status?" Mark asked. His smiley grey-blue eyes were filled with worry.

"His arm is broken. It's a miracle it wasn't worse. The doctor said we can take him home tonight."

The big door swung open again, and a nurse rolled Sam out in a wheelchair. His right arm was in a white plaster cast.

I crammed into the back of Mark's Fiat and Sam rode on Mom's lap in front. When we pulled into our driveway, the house was totally dark. Mark came in with us, and we turned on the lights in the living room.

Sam was sleepy because of the pain medicine they had given him at the hospital. Mark and Mom put him to bed.

"I'll call you in the morning, Michelle," Mark said. He gave her a hug then patted me on the back. "Good night, Thea."

"Good night," I said.

I was cold and so tired. I put on my nightie and climbed into bed. *Tap, tap, tap.*

"You still awake?" Mom opened the door, and the light from the hall streamed in around her silhouette.

"Yeah, Mom. Come in."

Mom sat on the side of my bed. "Thea, I just wanted to tell you that I'm so proud of you. Everything we've endured this last year—you've been a tremendous help—watching your little brother—"

"Oh Mom, I don't think I did too good a job watching my brother," I said.

"You and Sam have been playing in that old tree since you were big enough to climb it. I'm just grateful you were here to call for help when he fell." She paused. "I should have been—"

"No, Mom. I want you to go out and have fun."

"Thea, you are a godsend." She hugged me, and I cuddled up to her. "Everything is going to get better and better. That's what I believe. I told the police I don't want them to press charges against Ray."

"But what about everything he did?"

"I want him to get help. He's going to testify against that horrible Bruno character, and in exchange, Ray won't be prosecuted."

"Nothing will happen to him?"

"He's entering an alcohol treatment program, and he's going to live in a halfway house."

"Halfway to what?"

"Funny, Thea. It's a regular house, but with roommates and supervision. They receive help finding legitimate jobs. What good would it do to put Ray in prison? What's done is done. Anyway, if he doesn't clean up his life and live by the rules, the judge said he will send him to prison."

"Is he mad at me?"

"No, honey. Ray knows he brought all this on himself."

"He won't come around here, will he?"

"He wasn't always like this, Thea. Your dad loved him so much. So did Mamac." She sighed. "You don't get to pick your family. He's still one of us."

"Sam and I are mad at him. He's the reason Dad—"

"I know . . . ," Mom said.

"I wish Dad were here now. It's so unfair."

"I wish he were here too." Mom's voice cracked, and she cleared her throat.

"I didn't mean to—"

"It's not you, Thea. It's—when I came home tonight and saw Sam laid out on that stretcher, I felt like my heart was being ripped out of my chest. It reminded me of—"

"What?"

"The day I came home and found your dad. The

paramedics carried him out of the house and put him in an ambulance—just like tonight. You and Sam were at school, thank goodness."

"I miss Dad so much."

"I know, honey. I do too. Mamac used to say, 'If you jump off a cliff, you better have wings or a soft place to land.' We've leapt and landed—the three of us—on soft ground."

"I don't remember Mamac saying that. She talked about leaping and having wings—as in flying?"

Mom smiled. "Once in a while. It was just an expression she used."

"Mom, everyone else's family is so—normal. Two parents, no moving around, no houses on fire, no bad uncles. Look at Angela—"

"Other people's families look better when you're on the outside looking in. Would you want to be Angela? Her mother—"

"I wouldn't trade you for any mother in the whole world, especially Angela's."

"Honey, I'm sorry I had to go to work and couldn't be home more for you."

"No, Mom. It's not like that. You are a great Mom. It's okay that you work. You do everything for us."

"I love you so much, Thea."

"I love you too, Mom."

Mom went out, shutting the door softly behind her. I snuggled under my rosebud duvet and slipped into a dreamless slumber.

Two Weddings, Two Babies

Sam loved the attention he got for his broken arm. Everyone signed his cast, and Sam made bad, left-handed drawings all over it.

I tried not to think about the invisible staircase, but I did think about it. I thought about it every day. Finally, I couldn't stand it anymore.

One evening, after dinner, I slipped out the back door and walked briskly down the brick path. I rounded the back of the garage, sprinted across the dichondra, and slipped through the willow's silvery-green curtain.

I ran to the willow and vaulted into the crook where the trunk forked, then I climbed the left side.

Up and up I went until I was just below where the invisible staircase had been. The raw, splintered nub—all that was left of the branch Sam had broken—was just above me. *Poor tree. Sam snapped off one of its arms.*

I leaned on the trunk and stood up, then I looked down. The ground was a dizzy distance. *Don't think about falling.* Because of the broken branch, there was little to hold onto. I concentrated on staring straight ahead. Placing one foot in front of the other, I walked the limb like a balance beam and stretched one arm above my head as high as I could. *Just a little farther.* I reached, waving at the sky. Nothing. *One more step—just to make sure.* I batted the air. No ledge. No staircase.

I picked my way down the tree and sat cross-legged amidst the twigs and sticks that still littered the ground from Sam's fall. *It's gone. And Mamac . . . I won't ever see her again.*

I never told Sam I'd gone back up the tree, and he never asked.

*A*ngela sent me a postcard from Hawaii. She said it was "fabulous," and she was on her way to Boise for the remainder of summer.

In September, I started seventh grade at Jefferson Junior High. I hadn't heard from Angela, so I called her old number. It was disconnected. When I called the operator and asked for her new number, she said it was unlisted. The Valley seemed very far away—like a foreign country.

At my new school, I found some of the kids I had known from Pacific Palisades Elementary—the school I went to before we moved to Mar Vista. I joined the volleyball team and made new friends too. Seventh grade chugged along, and Mamac's house felt more and more like home.

Mark came over every week. I liked him okay because Mom smiled and said, *yes,* when he was around. He started taking Sam to buy matchbox cars. Sam loved that. Together, they doubled the size of his collection.

In June, Mom gave me twenty dollars to shop for summer clothes. I took the bus, all by myself, to the mall at Pico and Westwood Boulevards.

I was standing inside the May Co. when I noticed a woman in a white dress. She was flipping through hangers on a clothes rack, selecting dresses as she went, and piling them on the blonde girl whose arms were already full.

"Angela!"

Angela dropped her load on the floor and ran toward me, squealing with delight.

"Thea!" She hugged me.

Mrs. V stepped over the pile, unconcerned about the mess. "Thea, is that you? How stunning you are! What a lovely physique." She looked me up and down. "Angela, look at your old school chum. She is quite svelte. You are such a sausage!"

Angela blushed and looked away.

"I have an idea," Mrs. V said. "Let's take a hiatus. I want to give your father a jingle anyway."

Before we could answer, she was headed for the exit. "Orange Julius—how fortuitous! You girls may enjoy a beverage and have a little *tête-à-tête.*"

Angela and I sat at the counter and ordered. Heads turned as Mrs. V bustled out of the Orange Julius. Her high heels made a clapping sound on the tile floor. It sounded like someone was applauding her.

Angela said, "Our new house in the Valley is so big. I

am going to the Ivy Bound Academy now. It is a private institution for students aspiring to Ivy League universities. Oh my goodness. It is not correct to speak solely about oneself. Please, Thea, tell me about you."

"Sam broke his arm last summer. He couldn't wait to climb the willow again. He went too high and bam! The branch broke."

"How frightening."

"You're telling me. I almost had a heart attack. I thought he was dead or something."

"Dreadful."

"So, Angela, the invisible staircase—Sam looked—before the branch broke. I climbed the willow one more time after that too. It's not there. No more dreams either. No more . . ," I hadn't said her name in a while, "Mamac. I thought you'd want to know."

"You are so amusing, Thea. That was just a game we played. Why are you telling me this?"

"I'm talking about—flying."

"I do not believe in silly things like that. You are so—well, immature."

Mrs. V appeared outside the glass door. She was walking toward us and digging through her big red purse. Sweat trickled down my back and the fluorescent lights of the Orange Julius shop made the room appear overexposed. I felt nervous and foolish. My friend wasn't my friend, and our adventure wasn't our adventure.

"But Angela, don't you remember?"

"Of course I do! We played make-believe in that old tree in your grandmother's garden."

Mrs. V swung the glass door open and entered. Her

heels clapped and customers stared.

"But the staircase—" I whispered. I was begging.

"Not real. Stop it now, I—"

"There you are," Mrs. V cooed. She pulled some bills out of her purse and slapped them on the counter. "Time to go, Angela. So lovely to see you, Thea."

"I am ready," Angela said, sliding off her stool.

"Would you—can I—I could call you," I said.

"I am so very busy. Do you have the same number as before?"

"No. We have Mamac's number now."

"We have the number, darling," Mrs. V said. "Our summer plans are a whirlwind."

"Okay," I said, wanting to believe Angela would call but knowing she wouldn't.

I went to the glass door and watched them promenade down the mall. Mrs. V pointed at a window display of mannequins in chic dresses. Angela looked wherever her mother directed and nodded.

*M*om and Marc got married that August. It was a small wedding in a white church by the ocean in Santa Monica. Mario Lomax was best man, and Sam and I stood at the altar too. Mom held a bouquet of purple and yellow irises.

I had the same bouquet, only smaller. Mark, Mario, and Sam wore boutonnieres on the lapels of their jackets—a single yellow-and-purple iris. Olive Dancer came, but Uncle Ray wasn't invited.

"God bless you, Michelle," Olive Dancer said after the ceremony. "Mary Ann is smiling in heaven. May she rest in peace."

Mark's parents invited me and Sam to stay with them so Mom and Mark could go on their honeymoon without us, but Mark said, "No way. The four of us are going to have a blast."

We drove to Baja California and camped on San Felipe Beach. I learned to snorkel in the ocean, and we made a campfire every night.

When we returned home, Mark moved into Mamac's house with us.

On Sunday, a couple of weeks later, the doorbell rang. When I opened the door, I almost fainted! I thought I was looking at Dad. A man with neatly cut, brown hair and striking dark eyes stood on the doorstep.

"Hi, Thea," Uncle Ray said. "Your mom invited me."

Mom and Mark made chicken salad sandwiches for lunch. We all sat at the maple table.

I didn't feel hungry, and Sam didn't touch his food. He sat, staring at Uncle Ray. I kicked him under the table to get him to stop.

"So, how have you been?" Mom asked.

"I need loads of help. I can't do it alone. No one can. I need forgiveness from so many people—all of you guys to start with—but also from God. I need to learn grace—to be better, not bitter. Hey, I just made that up. I could put it on a bumper sticker. *Be Better, Not Bitter.*"

"Good one, Ray," Mark said.

"But seriously, there is so much to be thankful for in this world. Just being alive is so amazing." A heavy silence fell on the room, and everyone thought about Dad. Uncle Ray had put his big fat foot in his big fat mouth. He stopped chewing, and his eyes welled with tears.

"Let's take a walk," Mark said. He led Ray out the front door, and they took off down the sidewalk. I went to the living room window and watched. Mark was talking and gesturing with his hands. Uncle Ray was walking with his hands in his pockets, listening.

I thought about the day I met Angela. *We sat under the willow tree and ate mashed avocado with garlic salt on toast. The day I told her my secret promise. I was going to find out who shot Dad, and he was going to pay for it. And I did find out. Uncle Ray didn't shoot Dad— that bad man, Bruno, did. Now he's in jail. But Uncle Ray was the reason Dad got shot. So . . . why is Uncle Ray visiting us? Why did Mom invite him?*

Mom came over and put her hand on my shoulder. "Is this hard for you, Thea?"

"What?"

"Having your uncle here?"

"Well, sort of. I mean, how can you be nice to him? He's the reason—"

"There, but for the grace of God, go I."

"What?"

"It means, we all start out as innocent babes. Ray got on the wrong track and needs help. Just about everyone deserves a second chance. I'd like Ray to do well in life, in spite of everything."

"But what about Dad?"

"Ray was into a bad way of living, and when your dad died, I thought Ray might be involved. When you told me you heard him say, 'I'm sorry,' and, 'it's all my fault,' at your dad's funeral, it confirmed my hunch. For two years I suffered in silence. Ray wouldn't talk, and the police couldn't do anything. The night Ray came over and confessed the truth to us, is the night my healing began. I could have chosen to hate Ray, but instead, I gave myself a huge gift."

"What gift?"

"The gift of forgiveness. It hurts me more than anyone to stay angry. If I forgive Ray, I'm helping myself. I know it's what your dad would want. It's hard to explain, Thea. It's part of accepting what happened. It's what allowed me to get remarried. I'm choosing love."

"I get it, Mom."

*O*n a different Sunday, we were making our traditional pancake breakfast on Mamac's pink stove. It had a griddle built into its top, and Sam was standing on a step stool, flipping pancakes when the doorbell rang. Mark went to answer it. A moment later, Uncle Ray was standing in the kitchen doorway.

"You're getting to be a pro at that Sam," Uncle Ray said.

"You have to wait till the bubbles pop, then you know it's time to flip 'em." Sam slid the spatula under a pancake, and with a snap of his wrist, sent it into the air. It landed with a plop, halfway off the griddle, splashing pancake mush onto the stove burner. "Oops," he said.

"No shame there, buddy. Takes a long time to be a professional pancake flipper. I admire your effort."

We sat down to eat, and Uncle Ray said, "Best pancakes I ever tasted. Cooked to perfection."

Sam grinned with self-satisfaction.

"How are things going?" Mom asked.

"The people at church have been so good to me," Uncle Ray said, his mouth stuffed with pancakes. "I'm going to show everyone that I can make good with my life."

After that, it seemed like Uncle Ray came for brunch every Sunday. A few months later, Uncle Ray said to me, "Hey, Thea. In case you're wondering, I'm not mad at you."

"Mad at me?"

"You know, for breaking into my house, getting the cops after me, not to mention burning my arm."

He showed me the underside of his right arm. Midway between his wrist and elbow, there was a shiny scar about the size of a dime where I had ground out the burning cigarette.

"I guess . . ." My face and ears felt hot, and before I could think of what to say, Uncle Ray grabbed me and gave me a big hug.

"I'm joking, Thea. What you kids did that day forced me to face the mess I had made of my life." He released me and looked me in the eye. "Thank you."

"You gonna thank me too?" Sam asked.

Uncle Ray grabbed Sam and turned him upside down, holding him by the ankles. "I'm checking to see if any quarters you stole off my dresser fall out of your pockets."

"I didn't steal any quarters," Sam shouted. His face was beet red, and his hair hung to the floor. "We were looking for your stinky gasoline."

Uncle Ray gently laid Sam on the floor. Then he helped him stand up and smoothed Sam's hair back into place. "I know. Just another one of my dumb jokes. You kids saved me from myself. Thank you, Sam."

That evening, Sam asked me, "Do you like Uncle Ray

coming over?"

"Do you?"

"I kind of like him, but he did all that bad stuff."

"He's trying to be the person he was supposed to be—before he totally messed up."

"Yeah. He's different now. Before, he was like—a werewolf."

I laughed. "Mamac and Dad loved him. Mom is trying to forgive him . . . .

*I*n May, nine months after Mom and Mark got married, my sister, Clementine, was born.

Clementine didn't look like Sam and me. She had curly blonde hair and big blue eyes. She was the glue that made our new family real, and fun, and happier than it had been in a long time.

I was finishing eighth grade. For the first time since Dad died, I felt good in my own skin. I belonged in this world. I was Thea MacRobert—daughter of Howard and Michelle MacRobert, stepdaughter of Mark Brightwell. I was the granddaughter of Mary Ann MacRobert. I was the big sister of Sam and Clementine. I was me, and I liked that.

Life marched along: school, volleyball, friends, vacations. Another summer. Another school year.

Mark liked to have barbecues in the backyard. Mom kept inviting Uncle Ray and, little by little, having him around felt normal.

One Saturday afternoon when I was in tenth grade, Ray showed up for barbecue with a blonde woman.

"Everybody, this is Julie," he said, grinning hugely.

"But she's so pretty," Sam declared. Everyone laughed. Sam was twelve years old, but he still had a talent for saying stupid things.

Julie blushed.

"We met at the singles group at church," Uncle Ray said.

"Ray, you're just a late bloomer," Mom kidded. "Welcome, Julie."

"I may be a late bloomer, but I have found the prettiest flower in the entire state of California. I want you all to know, Julie and I are getting married."

Uncle Ray's announcement was a total surprise. But before long, Julie became a part of our family too. You couldn't help but love her. She laughed easily and was a naturally cheerful person. She'd bring little gifts for me and Sam: straw finger pulls, clapper balls on a cord, card tricks—stuff like that. She loved holding Clementine, and she'd walk around with her on her hip. You could hardly pry the kid out of her arms. When she wasn't holding Clementine, she was playing tag with me and Sam. She'd laugh and chase us, or we'd chase her, and she usually let Sam tag her.

Julie and Uncle Ray got married. A year later, they had their own little girl. She was born in December, and they named her Holly.

*T*en years had passed since Mamac died. It was our last summer in her house. In a few weeks, the house would be turned over to Uncle Ray, just as Mamac had written in her will. Mom, Mark, and Clementine were moving a few miles away to Santa Monica, near Mark's parents.

Sam was eighteen, and I was twenty-two. I had just finished college in Northern California, and Sam had just graduated high school. In September, he planned to fly clear across the country, to New York, to attend college.

It was a warm August evening. We had just eaten barbecued steak. Mom, Mark, and Clementine had gone into the house to clean up. Sam and I were being lazy, lounging on lawn chairs in the twilight. "Hey, Sam, I've been thinking—"

"Holy moly. Clear the decks! Thea's been thinking," Sam kidded.

I swatted the air between us, pretending to hit him. "Hilarious. Really, Sam. I have been thinking—" Sam laughed, and I couldn't help but laugh too. "Will you stop it? I want to tell you something."

"Do tell." He rested his chin on the palm of his hand and stared at me cross-eyed.

I ignored his clowning. "For us—you and me—this is the end of an era. The end of our home—here at Mamac's." Sam's smile evaporated, and he leaned back in his chair. "Uncle Ray gets Mamac's house now—permanently. Coming here will never be the same. It won't be our home, our gathering place."

"You sure have a knack for taking the fun out of a perfectly nice evening," he said.

"Sorry."

"Anyway, I know, Thea. Believe me, I know."

We sat in silence.

"You're going to have a blast in New York. I'm jealous. Wish I had gone out of state for college."

"True that, sis. Big plans ahead. New York City, here I

come."

"I'm going to miss you, Sam."

"Really? Thought you'd be glad to be rid of me."

"You're a riot this evening, Mr. Smarty Pants. I feel like we are saying goodbye to our childhood. We probably won't ever climb the willow again."

Sam laughed. "Last time I did that, I fell and almost killed myself."

"Right, but I was thinking about the old days. You know," I lowered my voice even though no one else was around, "the invisible staircase, the night we—"

"The old days? You mean the really old days."

"Yes, right after Mamac died. What we did—"

"You've been thinking about your flying stories."

"Flying stories?"

"Yeah, you told me there was an invisible staircase at the top of the willow tree. It was you, me, and that blonde chic. You know, the one with the uptight mother."

"Angela," I said, staring at him in the fading light. "Sam?"

"What?"

"Those weren't stories."

Full Circle

Sam laughed. "Yeah, right—not stories."

"No one is listening. We came here at midnight—and climbed the willow—and found the staircase—and flew."

"I remember coming here in the dark. I was terrified. That was so insane."

"You were only eight. You followed us in your bathrobe!"

"True that. I couldn't be left out. No way."

"But Sam. You must remember what we did that night."

"I remember hiding in the tree and waiting for the fire trucks. I think those games started after I told you I had that dream about Mamac, right after she passed away."

"Wait a minute, Sam. I was the one who had the dream—not you! You never told me you had a dream about Mamac."

Sam rolled his eyes. "Yes, I did—the dream about the

lady with the psychedelic pink lights. She was floating above the willow, then she kind of glided, like she was coming down an invisible staircase. I remember 'cause you told me it was a vision of Mamac."

"I don't want to go to bed! I want Thea and Sammy." Eight-year-old Clementine came running down the back steps of the house, hollering at the top of her lungs. She raced down the brick path and jumped into Sam's lap.

Our last weekend at Mamac's, Mom gave a party. She invited Uncle Ray and his growing family. Uncle Ray and Julie now had two children—Holly, five, and Howie, three.

Mom hugged Uncle Ray when he came in the front door. "Mamac would have been so pleased to see you with your beautiful family." Mom hugged Julie too. "This is your home now. The four of you need it more than we do. I know you will make many happy memories here."

"Who's ready for a burger?" Mark asked as he headed out the back door.

Everyone followed. We squeezed onto the benches of the picnic table, and three-year-old Howie sat on Julie's lap. After we ate, Holly chased Clementine in and out of the drooping limbs of the willow tree, and Howie ran as fast as he could (which was pretty fast), trying to catch them.

Julie was as fun as ever. Her smile was contagious, and her energy seemed boundless. "Excuse me," she said to the grown-ups at the table. She stood up and walked stiffly toward the children in her most dramatic Frankenstein march. "I'm still hungry. I'm going to eat all of you!" she said in her scary-monster voice. The children screamed and scattered.

*T*he following year, I married James, my college sweetheart. His family was from Sonoma in Northern California, and that's where we made our home—four hundred miles north of Los Angeles. We wanted to start a family as soon as we could, and a year later, our little girl was born. We named her Rose Elizabeth (because I loved Mamac's Queen Elizabeth roses).

At five years old, Rose was a rugged tomboy. She hated dresses, collected yo-yos, and ran the streets with the neighborhood boys—climbing trees, playing ball, and getting scraped up and dirty.

James would complain, "Can't you encourage that girl to be more, you know, like a girl?"

"She is who she is, James. There are all kinds of girls."

Most evenings, I would lay down with Rose at bedtime and tell her stories. We didn't need a reading light because they were my stories, and they didn't come from books.

I told stories about Mamac: Christmas dinners, Easter egg hunts, Mamac baking bread, her pink house, her pink refrigerator, and her pink roses. There were stories about Dad: the summer we went camping in Yosemite (and the bear that ate our dinner), Sunday morning pancake breakfast, running into Dad's arms, and him catching me, and swinging me in a circle.

I also told Rose stories about the willow tree: an enchanted cameo brooch, an invisible staircase, and three children who flew. Every time I took out the old memories, dusted them off, and told them to Rose, they changed slightly. Rose noticed this, and sometimes, she remembered the details better than I did.

"Mommy, tonight tell me a flying story."

"Angela and I went down the brick path to the willow tree—"

"No, Mommy, Uncle Sammy was there too. He was in his brown bathrobe and matching slippers. Angela made him go up the tree last."

"Oh, right, Uncle Sammy was there too. He was afraid of the dark, so he walked between us. Angela was mad about that, so when we got to the tree, she made him go up last."

$\mathcal{M}$y life in Sonoma was great. James had a big family, and Rose had an assortment of aunts, uncles, and cousins. Every summer and Christmas break, we visited my family at Mom and Mark's house in Santa Monica. Sam had made New York his permanent home. He was a big shot in the New York Stock Exchange, but he came to California when he could and always made it for Christmas.

The same year Rose was born, Uncle Ray and Julie had a third baby—a boy they named Alex. The kids loved it when we visited. With Uncle Ray's three kids, plus Rose and Clementine, they were a rolling ball of laughter, boo-boos, quarreling, and constant mess. Clementine, being the oldest, liked to be the leader. She was good at it, except when she became too bossy. Rose loved Alex the most. They were the same age and were like brother and sister, except they didn't fight.

The five kids would stay outside past dusk, running up and down the block playing hide-and-seek. Every few minutes, we heard someone calling, "Ollie ollie oxen, free

free free."

When it got dark, James would start to worry. He'd stand on the front steps, shouting, "Kids, come in! It's dark. Come in right now!"

*E*very year, to celebrate her birthday, Rose had three parties: one with her friends, one with James' family, and a third celebration with just James and me.

When Rose turned eight, she requested angel food cake with whipped cream and strawberries for her party with James and me. We had each just eaten a big piece, and it was time for presents. Rose tore them open: shin guards for soccer, a basketball, a zip line. There was one present left. It was wrapped in pink tissue paper.

"Rose, you may be a little young to wear this, but I want you to have it."

Rose unwrapped the paper and recognized the silver heart-box that usually sat on my dresser.

"Cool," she said. "Is the you-know-what inside?"

I nodded.

Rose opened the box and removed the cameo. "This is for me, Mommy?" Her hazel eyes blazed with excitement.

"Yes, if you'd like it. It's a family heirloom. You'll need to keep it in its box when you're not wearing it."

Rose jumped out of her chair and gave me a big hug. "I didn't know it was an ear-loom, Mommy."

"Heirloom, honey," James corrected. "That means it's been in Mommy's family for a long time."

"I know that. It's the magic cameo that Mamac gave Mommy."

"Magic?" James looked at me inquisitively.

"Didn't Mommy tell you about Mamac's magic cameo, Daddy?"

"It's from our bedtime stories. I'll explain later," I said, blushing.

"This is my favorite present," Rose declared.

"Why is that, sweetie?" James asked.

"Because of Mamac and the magic."

Rose's face blurred through the tears that filled my eyes. My heart was full. I had the most precious reasons for living, right here at my kitchen table—a husband that I loved and a child we loved together.

"Can I wear it now?" Rose asked.

"Of course you can." I pinned it on her shirt, and she ran to the bathroom to look in the mirror.

I felt James staring at me. Unspoken questions shot from his eyes like little darts. I avoided his gaze. James knew everything about my life. Everything—except the big thing.

I had wanted to tell James about Mamac appearing in my dream after she died, about the invisible staircase, the flying. I had tried a few times, but I just couldn't do it. James was so down-to-earth. He wouldn't have believed me. No. My memories were safe as long as they stayed in my head and were only shared as bedtime stories.

A year later, Rose was finishing fourth grade. She played spring and fall soccer and was such a good runner, they made her midfielder.

James taught language arts at Sonoma High School, and I enjoyed being at home. I had missed my mom when she worked, and I wanted to be there when Rose came home from school. I liked taking her to soccer practice and making dinner every night.

"Let's take a vacation to Mexico—just the two of us," James would say.

"No, James. We can't leave Rose."

"She can stay at your mom's. She loves it there."

"When she's a little older," I would say.

James was elated the day I said, "I've been thinking about that trip to Mexico. Rose is nine now. She could stay at my mom's for a week."

"Yes!" James exclaimed.

"I admit, I am protective of Rose. She is my only child. I can't help it."

"She'll be fine. She'll have Clementine. However, isn't Clementine about sixteen now? Rose would probably prefer to stay at Ray and Julie's so she can play with Alex."

"She can't stay at Mamac's."

"What?"

"I mean, she can't stay at Ray and Julie's." I laughed but felt nervous.

"All righty," James replied. "And that's because . . . ?"

"Alex may come and visit, but I want Rose at Mom's where we know she's safe."

"Whatever makes you happy, sweetie. I'm just glad to go away with you."

I called Mom. She checked with Mark. He agreed, and it was settled. Come June, we were off to Puerto Vallarta, and Rose was off to Grandma Michelle's.

But here's how life works: when you turn things over to others, they are no longer under your control. James and I had our week of sun and fun in Puerto Vallarta.

When we returned, we flew into Los Angeles International Airport and picked up our car in the long-term parking lot. We went straight to Mom's house to pick up Rose, and I found her in the kitchen, helping Clementine make cookies. The first thing I noticed was the cameo. It was pinned to her green T-shirt, which was smeared with cookie dough.

"The cameo!" I said, more forcefully than I meant to.

Rose stared at me, not comprehending.

"How did it get here?" I said.

"I brought it, Mommy. What's wrong?"

"Nothing. I just didn't know you had it with you." *It's fine,* I told myself. *It's hers to wear. Good grief, Thea. Calm down.*

On the drive back home, I asked Rose how her week had gone.

"Fun! Grandma Michelle let me sleep over at Uncle Ray and Aunt Julie's. Me and Alex made a fort with sheets under a big tree in the backyard. It had a rug and Christmas lights, and we plugged them at night.

My stomach lurched. I wanted to say, *What happened? Tell me everything!*

"Alex and I," James corrected.

"No, Daddy. You weren't there," Rose said.

"You slept outside under a tree?" I asked.

"No, Mommy. Daddy was with you. He didn't sleep outside with us."

"Rose, I only meant to say *me and Alex* is not correct. One should say *Alex and I*. Got it?" James said.

Rose laughed. "I thought you were mixed up, Daddy. *Alex and I* slept in the fort two whole nights. Then

Grandma Michelle said it was time to go back to her house."

It was a long drive back to Sonoma—about seven hours. We brought food from Mom's and stopped only for potty breaks. It was dark when we pulled into our driveway. Rose had fallen asleep in the back seat.

It felt good to climb into my own bed, but I slept fitfully. Worrisome thoughts jammed my mind. *Did Rose and Alex climb the willow? Rose could have fallen! Alex could have fallen! But they didn't fall. Did Rose wear the cameo when she slept over there? Did Mamac appear? Did Rose and Alex find the invisible staircase? After Sam fell out of the tree, the invisible staircase went away. But I know it was real. Angela and Sam denied the whole thing, but I know what we did. Angela and I did meet in our dream. We did see Mamac. We climbed the tree. We flew. Then we went back with Sam and did it again.* My ruminations swirled like smoke. Finally, in the wee hours of dawn, I fell into a deep sleep.

The next day, we unpacked from our trip. In the afternoon, James and Rose went to the grocery store, and I made lasagna and salad for dinner.

All day I had wanted to ask Rose about the sleepover under the willow. When we sat down for dinner, I said, "So, how was your stay with Grandma Michelle?"

"Gooood," Rose said as she stuffed salad into her mouth. "How was Mexico?" Her mouth was so full that lettuce shot out when she spoke. She laughed, and lettuce dribbled onto her plate.

James and I laughed too. It felt great to be together again.

At bedtime, I asked Rose, "Would you like me to tell you a story tonight?"

"Yes, Mommy. Of course!"

I turned out the light and left the door ajar like I always did. The light from the hall made the light fixture on the bedroom ceiling splay long shadows across the ceiling and wall. I lay down next to Rose.

"What story shall I tell tonight?" I asked.

"About the willow tree, Mommy."

"All right," I said in a casual voice. "Once, there was a little girl. Her grandmother, whom she called Mamac, passed away, and the little girl missed her very much. One night, the little girl had a dream—"

"No, Mommy, not like that," Rose said. "Like this: there were two children—a boy and a girl. One night, they slept under a willow tree. The little girl had a magic cameo, and it lighted up when it got really nighttime."

My heart began to race. "Okay," I said. "There were two children, a boy and a girl, who slept under a willow tree. The little girl had a magic cameo that lit up. Then, high above the tree, a woman in a sparkling dress appeared."

"Did she speak to the boy and girl, Mommy?"

"She saw them, but she never—"

"Yes, she did, Mommy. She spoke to them. She said, 'Come. Climb the tree. There is something here for you. Something you will like.'"

"Right," I said. "She said, 'Climb the tree,' like you said, Rose."

"So, they did climb the tree, and found the invisible staircase, and flew all around the neighborhood." Rose raised her hand and swooped the air in the dim light, demonstrating. "When they got back, the sparkly lady was still there. She was waiting."

"She was?" I said.

"Yes, she was. And you know what she said?"

"What?"

"She said, 'The greatest secrets are hidden in places you don't expect. People who don't believe will never find them.'"

"You know what, Rose? Uncle Sammy doesn't believe the invisible staircase is real."

"That's so sad, Mommy."

"He forgot what happened to us a long time ago. I think maybe it's my fault because, when we were kids, I told him it wasn't true."

I felt Rose's hand on my cheek. She turned my face so it was close to hers and looked into my eyes as she spoke. "Uncle Sammy didn't forget. When he has a little boy or a little girl, he will tell them bedtime stories, and he will remember."

"I hope so," I said.

"But Mommy, I want to tell you something else."

"Tell me something else."

"The lady in pink said that when you love someone really a lot, and they die, they don't really die. I mean, they do, but they are here and here." Rose touched my forehead and my heart. "As long as you remember."

"Hmmm," I murmured.

"Mommy?"

"Yes, Rose?"

"Children can climb the willow and find the invisible

staircase, but grown-ups can't, right?"

"Right." I chuckled but felt a twinge of longing.

"The lady said she came because of the cameo, but she won't come anymore. And the staircase won't be there anymore, but—"

"But—" I said, listening intently.

"Mommy, she said . . . She said to tell you—"

"Tell me?"

"Yes. Please don't interrupt me. She said, 'Tell your mommy, I am waiting for her in the same place she found me when she was little.' That's what she said. And she also said, if you want, sometimes you can go there. You know how. You fall backward in your head—into the green light —before you go to sleep. That's the place where you will find her. She will always be there—loving you. That's what she said."

"I love you, Rosie."

"I love you too, Mommy." Rose draped her arm around my neck and settled her head on the pillow. In a moment, she was sound asleep.

Some may forget.
Some may remember.
Some may choose to forget,
and then, when they're all grown up,
be young enough at heart
to remember all over again.

It was a wild ride—
childhood, adolescence, adulthood.
I wasn't jealous of Rose.
I was grown up, just as I should be.
Magic is for children.
But love—that is for everyone.

❀ Thea MacRobert-Vidal ❀

About the Author

Cathleen Claussenius lives in Portland, Oregon with Cleopatra, a long-haired German Shepherd, and Tsuki, a feisty, old cat. Cathleen believes in the invisible staircase and wishes every child has someone in their life as dear as Mamac.

You may visit Cathleen at:
www.theinvisiblestaircase.com, or at:
www.moonlitmilepublishing.com.